The Italian Pleasures of Gabriele Paterkallos

by Pietros Maneos

The Italian Pleasures of Gabriele Paterkallos
1st Edition

About the Author:

Pietros Maneos, a graduate of The University of Miami, is the author of the poetry collections, *The Soul of A Young Man* and *Poems of Blood and Passion*. He currently resides in Florida.

ISBN 978-0-9852281-0-1

© 2012 – Pietros Maneos / Aesthete Press

Cover Art: Gabriela Gonzalez Dellosso

Cover Design: CulturalBook.com

The Italian Pleasures of Gabriele Paterkallos

A Novella in Letters

For Karen

There are only two distinct classes of men on earth, those who have strong feelings and those who despise them. – Madame de Staël

The following epistolary correspondence between Gabriele Paterkallos, an American poet in Rome to publish his first poetry collection, and Odysseus Pane, the esteemed, self-exiled American novelist residing in Paris, was surreptitiously purloined from Mr. Pane's apartment by one of his lovers and subsequently sold to me for a seven figure sum, whereupon I in turn sold the exclusive rights to Aesthete Press.

Upon hearing of my intention to publish these letters, both Mr. Paterkallos and Mr. Pane threatened my life to such an extreme degree that I have sought a permanent restraining order against both men, and am so fearful for my safety that I change location every few weeks. I do hope that in time their impassioned animus will subside, but this seems unlikely, so I would like the world to know in no uncertain terms that should I perish in some sort of questionable circumstance, Mr. Pane or Mr. Paterkallos is the culprit. So, without further ado, I present these letters to you, the general public.

-Jean Michel Baudelaire

It should be noted that just three weeks after penning the previous paragraphs for publication Mr. Baudelaire was found floating beneath the *Pont Neuf* in an apparent suicide. The police continue to investigate the matter but so far have no evidence to indicate that his unfortunate death was anything other than a suicide. The present whereabouts of Mr. Pane and Mr. Paterkallos remain unknown, but we have heard various rumors that they have been sighted in such far-flung locales as Dubai, Algeria, and Mongolia.

-The Editors of Aesthete Press

May 27th, 2001

Dearest Odysseus, many-nymphed,

I have received the official word from *'Bella Poesia'* in Rome, Italy, that they are planning to publish my poetry collection, *The Soul of A Young Man*, in January of 2002! I've decided to take advantage of my 'buona fortuna' by spending the entire summer traveling throughout Italy, with the option of withdrawing from the fall semester so as to extend my 'Grand Tour.' How exciting! I've always dreamt of exploring Italy, devouring both travel books about modern Italy as well as ancient histories of glorious Rome. Depending upon your schedule, perhaps you could leave Paris for a bit, traveling to Bella Roma to visit me?

-Gabriele, Il Poeta Bella,

June 2nd, 2001

Dear Odysseus, stallion-breaker,

I am writing to you from the Miami Airport. My flight departs in one hour, so I am just passing the time reading a little and gazing at the endless procession of gorgeous Latin women – lithesome gazelles – galloping through this airport. Miami has been called the gateway to South America, but my god, it seems to be the gateway to Eden itself, with Eve after Eve tempting me with their bronzy flesh and fiery eyes, as if Medea possessed the immortal beauty of Aphrodite.

But I should cease gushing over these wild-eyed, soft-thighed women, since I am about to fulfill my lifelong dream of visiting Rome! I cannot wait to simply walk through the historic streets, streets once walked upon by Antony and Caesar! I must go now, since a Colombian woman has seated herself next to me, casting coquettish glances in my direction, glances that lash my soul like the lances of a grizzled Macedonian phalanx; now, she has begun playing with her long-flowing tresses, sending me further and further into ecstatic despair. Viva Colombia! Viva Roma! Ciao! Ciao!

-Gabriele, lover of Latin women,

June 4th, 2001

Dear Odysseus, Parisian flâneur,

Oh Rome! While in the taxi driving from Fiumicino towards the Eternal City, I felt as if I was closing in upon the rose-guarded garden of heaven itself, wondering if I would hear the very singing of the angels celebrating my arrival at the golden gates of St. Peter. Have I gone mad, Odysseus? Rome still remains the symbolic capital of Western civilization, despite what the damned moderns will tell you. Let them have New York and London, while we delight in the delicious light of Paris and Rome! Forza Roma! Vive La Paris!

I am settling into my publisher's apartment here in Rome on Viale Medaglio D'oro. What a poetic sounding street, and how fitting it is that I shall reside on the 'Street of the Golden Medal.' He is traveling in the Mediterranean this summer, so I have rented his apartment here for the time being. This residence will serve as a base to explore as much of Italy as time and money will allow.

I wish you had been able to see the Roman moon last night, for it shone like a bed of beryl bathed in elysian light – like the bronzed armor of strong-armed Hector – like wild wisps of silver floating in a sun-whipped ether. With the

Roman moon swaying in the sky above, and the eternal city spread out before me like the lovely wings of a spring butterfly, what is a man to do, but sigh for pleasure? I could not be happier Odysseus!

-Gabriele, the proud Roman,

June 6th, 2001

Dear Odysseus, of the Heroic Soul,

Today was a glorious day! I weight-trained for one hour, boxed for another, then double-verbed my *Ode to Gaius Julius Caesar* before indulging in a *ménage à trois* with two young Romanian nymphs. Yes, I did say 'Romanian' not 'Roman' as the working class girls here are largely comprised of eastern Europeans who have come to Roma in hopes of better economic conditions.

How I love this city, my friend, and wish that I could remain here forever and ever, never returning to America, but alas, this is but a fantasy. I would need a large sum of gold to do so, though I am beginning to feel that I would rather be a pauper in Rome than the King of New York.

-Gabriele, The Roman Prince,

June 9th, 2001

Dear Odysseus, creator of supreme Beauty,

When young dawn with her tresses of golden rose unfurled herself upon the horizon, I nearly wept from the wealth of beauty before me. The warm, comely light coupled with the presence of rose-scented Paola sent my soul into a flight of uncontrollable ecstasy. Paola Marmara, born and raised in the Eternal City, is one of my accumulating Roman lovers, and perhaps my favorite. She is a Roman woman to the core – beautiful, sensual, fiery, and temperamental; her aquiline nose gives her a distinctly aristocratic air, as if she is the long-lost daughter of a Roman emperor. Her high cheekbones and angular jawline, both set in stunning symmetry, are reminiscent of a pretentious high-fashion model, yet Paola possesses none of the haughty aloofness of these insipid creatures, and like most Romans is accessible and inviting.

Paola is sometimes extreme in her tastes, at times begging me to bite her lower lip when we are at 'play,' nearly fainting from the maddening sensation of pain-pleasure. Yet in quieter moments between us, Paola often informs me in gruff language, that were she ever to catch me with another woman, she would stab me in the abdomen; however, Paola is always very emphatic in expressing the fact that it will only be a flesh wound, not a mortal blow; just enough to teach me a lesson, but not deep enough to send me permanently to the house of death. Paola loves to pantomime her fearsome dagger-thrust, as if she were a champion gladiatrix taunting a trembling opponent in the Colosseum.

Then invariably, almost as if feeling guilty for her violent threats and thrusts, she tries to comfort me by kissing various spots on my stomach, healing the imaginary wounds with her passion-parted lips. But personally, I think that she is merely marking her territory, mapping out exactly where she plans to draw blood in the future. If Paola only knew that I was also sleeping with her sister and cousin. My god, the rivers of blood that would flow into the Tiber!

We are disciples not only of lust, but also of gluttony. After our fierce coupling, she prepares her favorite dish of 'cacio e pepe,' which is steadily becoming my favorite as well; it is typical Roman fare comprised of spaghetti, olive oil, black pepper and Pecorino Romano cheese peppered with a little bit of pasta water. Though it is a staple here in Rome, it is a rare delicacy in America. When one orders it at an 'Italian' restaurant in the states, the waiter generally just shrugs his shoulders, yells 'fuggedaboutit,' and looks as confused as if one has just spoken to him in an obscure Mandarin dialect.

Oh, how I adore watching Paola glide about the kitchen like a domestic goddess, intently assembling the pasta, like rose-eyed Hera preparing an ambrosial feast for ravenous Zeus. She cooks completely naked, softly singing arias from Rossini or Puccini for her own amusement. There are few things in this world more beautiful than watching a perfectly proportioned nude female body move in smooth-moving harmony, while singing opera. Perhaps only the pure-souled singing of a nightingale in the dark of night, a lucent flash of light in a solar eclipse, or a translucent butterfly wing fluttering in the Italian wind can compete with Paola's transfiguring radiance.

Her long-flowing, flowery hair – the shade of an autumnal leaf slowly spinning to the earth – cascades down her back, which is curved in the shape of a waning moon. Her lustrous tresses trail to just above her lovely 'dimples of Venus,' where the ilium and sacrum kiss, forming an erotic union: a ravine fit only for the honey of heaven – an impression impressed with sacred beauty – an indentation bearing the fingerprints of the holy trinity. When I stare upon them, hypnotized by their perfection, I have no other desire in this life, other than to lose myself in those twin gardens.

-Gabriele, citizen of Sybaris,

June 10th, 2001

Dear Odysseus, lord of the narghile,

Rome is not a city, but a palace! I am sitting here in St. Peter's square in the dusky twilight basking in the immortal beauty. The dome of St. Peter's is gleaming in the glimmering gloam as if Bramante adorned its body in flecks of amber, stars of silver, and shards of jasper. Rome is the most spiritual of cities, Odysseus. A man leaves his home behind to venture here so as to find his soul. No, on second thought, not 'to find his soul,' but 'to make his soul.' Yes, that is much more apropos.

Here in this holy polis, Odysseus, a man embarks upon a lifelong journey of self-realization. For me, Rome has engendered a fevered desire to make my life consequential in some way; living in the Eternal City, even for this short amount of time, has fired a burning ambition to become great, to have my name resound throughout the centuries to come. If I had remained in America, never traveling to Italia, being a successful careerist would have sufficed as a life well lived. Rome serves as both a comfort and an inspiration to those with the Romantic soul of an Artist or a Conqueror.

The Eternal City has also strengthened my resolve to pursue Beauty and Truth for the rest of my earthly existence, no matter the consequence of such a decision, no matter the opinion of family, friends, and society at large. This heterodox position firmly establishes me as an outsider within modern culture, for I stand not with the 99%, nor the 1%, but defiantly alone.

-Gabriele Bonaparte

June 11th, 2001

Dear Odysseus, wandering Hellene,

I had an experience this morning that I think will perfectly illustrate the difference between our contemporaries and us. I was being driven through the outskirts of Rome, and in my peripheral vision noticed what seemed to be thousands of majestic hawks flying in the sky. I could not pull my eyes from the beauty before me, being an avid lover of birds. The driver noticed my rapt gaze and laughed to himself.

I asked him what was so humorous, and he remarked that all of his other patrons complain about the stench emanating from the landfill, but that I was the only one to stare like a little child at the birds flying above. And in truth, Odysseus, I hadn't noticed the smell since I was so engrossed in viewing the varied flight of these regal birds, as their wondrous wings drifted in between teeming beams of light.

Their movements were so graceful and peaceful that the entire firmament seemed to be in total unison, as if a moving symphony, a dazzling intermezzo, a spellbinding adagio were in progress – conducted by the very hand of God. I had an urge to write a poem about their beauty, and even dreamt of how lovely it would be to transmogrify into a flying hawk, completely free, beholden to no man, god or government, drifting aimlessly like a wandering gypsy through the sun-blessed sky.

Now, were one of the small-souled moderns in this cab, they would have written a prosaic fragment about the vile stench, or gone even further, commanding the driver to stop the car, so that they could roll about in the excrement and refuse, writing from the very belly of the landfill. Let these men be prophets of the gutter, while we continue to sing of the heavenly hawk. I am not a man wearing rose-tinted glasses, Odysseus, as I am well aware of the degradation and ugliness in the world, yet I am also sensitive to the vast empires of beauty in the cosmos, so much so, that I long for a thousand lives to experience every single sensation of beauty.

-Gabriele, student of The Beautiful,

P.S. I am off to Florence tomorrow!

June 16th, 2001

Dear lion-hearted Odysseus,

Greetings, my brother in beauty! I was in a heroic fisticuff this evening in a Florentine piazza, and was victorious, of course! You are certainly well acquainted with my loathing of the English, especially the English that frequent Tuscany; these lifeless, insufferable buffoons trudge about Tuscany as if it is their personal fiefdom referring to it as *Chiantishire* with the modern Italians cast as their obedient serfs.

Well, as I was dining alone in Piazza della Signoria, reading Dante, in between copious drafts of wine and generous bites of capellini, I overheard an English 'Lord' – well, if he wasn't a Lord, he surely comported himself as one – abusing one of the waitresses, ordering her about, chastising her, and the like. The poor girl, no more than nineteen, was fighting back tears, and what is unforgivable my friend is that she was beyond beautiful: her profile stolen from one of the far-famed Renaissance paintings, her lush lips as full and luscious as Aphrodite's, and her soft, dewy skin brushed with sun-blushed bronze. Her raven tresses alone inspired such longings that I had to restrain myself from composing erotic verse on the soiled napkins fluttering about in the Italian wind.

So, after two minutes of enduring this fustian fool, I arose declaiming, *'Go back to England, you nouveau riche peasant!'* Now, nothing angers a member of English aristocracy more than aspersions like 'nouveau riche' and 'peasant,' as they pride themselves on both their refinement and their breeding. He then retorted, *'Ah, The Ugly American wishes to play the role of hero.'* It was dripping with sarcasm and irony, of course, as both are adored by the English, and Anglophiles, alike. I hit him squarely in the nose with a vicious right cross. Ah, the glory! His nose shattered immediately with his blood splattering onto his plate of pasta causing it to resemble a postmodern abstract painting fit for hanging in the MoMA or The Whitney; the yoke-colored perciatelli, the pale heaping chunks of garlic, the carmine-hued tomato sauce, and the swirling blood all intermingled in violent opposition, forming a mass of blazing color, and free-wheeling Dionysian curvature.

His wife who looked as if she were culled from a Golden Ivory film, or a Henry James novel (is there any real difference?), shrieked like a speared antelope, frantically yelling for help. As soon as the punch landed and I realized its full impact, I started to run, not from fear of this man, but from the prospect of suffering in an Italian prison. As I dashed off, I glanced back at the waitress who was staring at me with such an admixture of awe, gratitude, and desire. I could have had her right then and there, my friend, but alas, I feared an Italian prison more than I desired the taste of her ambrosial lips.

-Gabriele, The Hero,

June 17th, 2001

Dear Odysseus, child of Kalon,

The full moon this evening is as numinous as a golden chalice bathed in bougainvillea – its nimbus, lovely and luminous, is stenciled in virginal diamonds; but enough of my lunar reveries, let me now recount my day. I spent the morning and part of the afternoon in the Uffizi Gallery. I must first tell you that I rushed past the gothic altarpieces on display finding them primitive and revolting, especially after seeing such idealized Greco-Italian beauty in Italy thus far. I am not sure which I abhor more: the gothic sensibility or the modern one, and while I am on this topic, let it be known to all that I am officially done with modernity and with those whom subscribe to the sophistry of the lionized vandals. Let the rabble bow before the false idols of the age, I simply will not!

Rather, let me come to rest upon the marble-smooth breast of sculpted Venus, begging her for a single kiss. When you are in the Uffizi, it becomes obvious that this ancient sculpture not only captures the very essence of The Beautiful, but also inspired Botticelli's heavenly 'The Birth of Venus.' Ah, imagine crafting a poem or a novel, Odysseus, that aspired to express such loveliness; one would surely fail to achieve this herculean labor, but the pursuit alone is sublime and heroic. In this painting, Botticelli has married the beauty of nature, the mystery of myth, and the majesty of the human form on one canvas – imbuing our fallen world with a rare glimpse of the divine, with the dreams of his beautiful soul.

There are many other gems to see here with Michelangelo's vibrantly colored 'Doni Tondo,' Caravaggio's wildly emotive 'Medusa,' and Paolo Moraldo's haughty 'Warrior with Equerry,' resonating with me personally, but the artistic treasures are so vast that I hope to return in the near future, perhaps even taking a guided tour with a renowned art historian.   After leaving the gallery, I wandered through the streets and piazzas of Florence noting that they seemed filled more with foreign tourists than indigenous Italians, but I assume that this is only the case during the summer months.

-Gabriele, the Florentine,

June 18th, 2001

Dear Odysseus, heroic-hearted,

Tonight the Florentine moon is cast in a panoply of alabaster light, revealing its unsightly beauty. While Selene, the goddess of dreams and desire, is purring the pleasing hymns of Pan upon these Italian lands, stirring my soul into a nirvana of feeling.

Earlier today I toured the far-famed Boboli Gardens. There is something immensely soothing to the spirit to spend time in a garden, especially a garden as grandiose as this one. Sitting near a body of water simply adds to the picturesque grandeur: the sound of falling water resounding like a carefully composed symphony placed among the surrounding greenery elevates this verdurous wonderland from that of an idyll to a forgotten corner of heaven. I spent an hour sitting before the Neptune fountain, just watching the water tremble when kissed by the Florentine wind. The delicate movement of water is one of life's simple beauties, and I never tire of observing this pastoral phenomenon.

As I slowly walked past the row of bay trees, and various other evergreens such as cypress, olive and ilex, I became happily drunk on their fragrant scents. I was tempted to pluck a few vines – plaiting myself in a wild-growing garland like a victorious Grecian athlete returning to his homeland from hallowed Olympia. But, upon further thought, I decided against this since it would attract too much attention, and I desired complete solitary anonymity today losing myself in sylvan realms of beauty. Hiding myself in a remote corner, far removed from the other tourists, I seriously contemplated applying for a job here as a gardener so that I would never have to leave this lovely sanctuary. Do not laugh at me, Odysseus. I know that it seems a ludicrous proposition, but I can think of few men more blessed than those who can revel in this resplendence on a daily basis.

While strolling through the timeless pathways, I saw many hand-holding couples, which further reminded me of my failure in affairs of the heart, sending me into a minor bout of melancholia. My first love was taken by the Gods in a terrible automobile accident, while my second left me for 'disappearing within my thoughts too often,' being too much of a broody recluse; she would always exclaim in an exasperated tone, *Just what are you thinking about, Gabriele?'* But the Arcadian Eden where I presently found myself quickly ameliorated these depressing musings, jolting me back into feelings of boundless joy.

The denouement of a visit to the Boboli Gardens should certainly be the view that it offers of Florence and the Tuscan countryside. Towards the end of my stay, I was overcome with hunger, so I sat down on a bench to have my lunch. The splendid panorama in my privileged purview resembled a masterful landscape painting of an ancient Master serendipitously sprung to life. While I nibbled on my prosciutto sandwich, I gazed upon this seemingly supernal vista – the lush landscape, expansive and pensive, seemed to increase in loveliness with every passing second like a flower slowly unsheathing its petals to enjoy the joyous afternoon light. I was as happy as a buzzing bee flushed with lush nectar. Oh Florence! Oh Italy!

-Gabriele, lover of Nature,

June 19th, 2001

Dear Odysseus, of the soaring war-cry,

I did not see any of the sights of Florence today, as I spent it in bed with the American heiress, Lily Fitch. The physicality of the entanglement was pleasurable, but her personality is annoying and tiring, as she possesses a modern sensibility, finding Florence and Italy boring, missing her native New York. Ugh! I almost vomited in my lap when she uttered such ridiculous inanity. Who could long for New York, let alone even give it one moment of thought, when residing in Italy?

A woman should be pleasant and pretty, and while Ms. Fitch is certainly pretty, she is exceedingly unpleasant, longing at all times to be perceived as 'edgy.' Lily also has pretensions to Art, but let me be abundantly clear here – they are nothing more than pretensions; her shtick is to glue 'found objects' that she chances upon during her travels onto a canvas. Once they are firmly affixed, she then proceeds to splatter paint upon them in a haphazard manner. She has had several shows in New York partly due to her family's financial influence, and partly due to the barbarous taste of that polis.

Lily tried to engage me in spirited debate, bringing up modern painters and critics, but I would not give her the pleasure of an intellectual connection; this was to be my revenge. She assumed that I was here in Italy to model, and I left it at that, not divulging the real nature of my trip here, allowing her to bask in her presumed intellectual superiority, completely unaware that she was in the presence of an immortal genius. Not only am I a veritable genius, Odysseus, but I am something of a genius in its concealment, if I so choose.

It is much easier this way, for once a woman discovers the elevated state of my intellect, they hunger for some sort of emotional connection whereas I generally prefer to keep it completely carnal. If I had a desire to debate aesthetics, I would do it with you, Odysseus, not with this Lily Fitch. Eventually, she tired of my deliberate taciturnity, leaving in a huff, probably labeling me a 'pretty boy with no depth.' Ha! Let her have her self-assured false fantasy until the release of my masterpieces. Masterpieces, I tell you, masterpieces!

-Gabriele, the superficial pretty boy,

June 21st, 2001

Dear Odysseus, man of bold actions,

I am now back in Rome, the center of the cosmos, having left Florence, riding the train through Tuscany. I much prefer Rome to Florence, as I find Florence to be more European than Italianate, whereas Rome possesses the high culture of the European North, while still retaining the earthy, raw, impassioned sensibility of the Italians. When one is in Florence, one may as well be in Madrid, London, or Paris, but when in Rome, one knows without question that one is in Italy. Here – the fallen ruins of antiquity and the passion of the people inscribe themselves into one's soul like a meticulously crafted mosaic immune to aging and decay: forever beautiful, forever eternal.

The train ride from Florence to Rome was as beautiful as a fable peopled with poppies and princesses. I sat by the window and gazed at the picturesque Tuscan countryside, with its undulating hills speckled with sheaves of spangled light. After witnessing the pastoral beauty of Tuscany, how can one not long to bring forth similar beauty into the universe – to fill one's verse with the very songs of spring – the holy hymns of butterfly wings, the aurorean dancing of leaping dolphins, and the wild wind singing of all things

Olympian. There is so much beauty contained in the world that at times I weep from the realization that one day it will all fade, fade as the glinting twilight succumbs to the dominance of night.

Someday we will merely be food for worms, not experiencing such beauty any longer: the golden dawn with her finger-tips of twining rose, the wine-dark sea set aflame by empires of fiery constellations, the mellifluent sound of falling water in a lonely piazza, and the pure smile of a small child. Do you not find beauty to be utterly overwhelming, the provenance of so much pain, yet so much pleasure?

-Gabriele, The Tuscan Philosopher,

June 24th, 2001

Dear Odysseus, of the honied speech,

I came to Rome to study antiquity, not iniquity, but the last three days have been awash in a sea of seedy sensuality. I have been playing with as many Roman women as will have me, living on raw oysters and feminine kisses kissed with airy jasmine. You would certainly approve of my sybaritic existence, but I am becoming bored with the excesses of the flesh.   Perhaps I should leave Rome, venturing to Mount Athos to see if the cloistered monks there could save my soul, or in the very least, teach me Attic Greek.

Speaking of the Greeks, I have recently been in touch with a Greek fellow here who mentioned that the Cyprus situation is once again coming to a boiling point, with possible armed conflict on the horizon. He asked me if I would throw my support behind the Greek cause, and I replied, *'Certainly, so long as I am fighting for the ideals of*

Hellas, and not on behalf of the pale-faced Galilean.' The modern Greeks are so damned Byzantine, and will probably cast the entire conflict as Galilean contra Mahometan, and I for one will not shed a single drop of my blood in his name, but in the name of Hellas, I would die a thousand deaths. Let the demos then say, *'Here is one who fell for Greece.'* I can dream of no nobler end other than dying for the principle of love.

But now speaking on love, I must state to you that I have never been *half in love* with an easeful death, much preferring the prospect of a heroic death. What say you, Mr. Pane? Will you come to Cyprus to fight the Turks with me, should I adopt this noble cause, and actually do something with my damned life? Like Odysseus (Homer's Odysseus, not you) I am no one, and nothing, but I long to do something epic, something worthy of my ancestors. I promise to give you command of many men, if you come along for the adventure. If nothing else, we will die cloaked in 'kleos apthiton,' disproving Auden's famous saying, *'Poetry makes nothing happen.'*

-Gabriele, son of Sappho and Herakles,

June 26th, 2001

Dear Odysseus, the earth-shaker,

This afternoon, I walked in total solitude through the gorgeous environs of the Villa Borghese, reading a bit of Homer and D'Annunzio to pass the passing hours of idleness. While lost in Homeric dreams, I had an idea for a satirical poem targeting the entire Anglo-American literary establishment, from high culture *à la* Eliot to low culture *à la* Bukowski, Ginsberg, and various other 'barbaroi.' I will model it on Byron's *'English Bards and Scotch Reviewers,'* hurling my 'dory' with precision, eviscerating my adversaries!

It will be an argument against minimalism, nihilism, and anti-aestheticism so revered by our contemporaries; it will restore *To Kalon* to its proper position in culture. Only a fool, a madman, or a genius would have the audacity to undertake such a bold project. Shall I begin to pen it, or should I simply occupy myself with the endless supply of Roman nymphs coming and going (with more comings than goings, of course) into my athenaeum?

The moon last night was positively spectacular, Odysseus. It was curled in the shape of a woman's lower lip in the very moment of ecstasy. And speaking of nymphs, I wrote this while Flavia slept beside me as I gazed upon the silver-glazed moon, whose wan light caressed the proud crest of Rome.

There's a whore on my right
And she'll be here all night
Even when I begin to write
Under the glorious Italian moonlight!

Now, I'm sure all of the feminazis will try to emasculate me for such sexism, but I use the term 'whore' not in the pejorative, but in its literal definition, as I paid Flavia for her company. Those who are acquainted with my predilections are well aware that I am a philogynist, not a misogynist. I'm not too concerned about the matter, however, as I am quite certain that the immortal Camille Pugliese will come to my defense against the assembled rabble of middling minds.

-Gabriele, student of The Beautiful,

June 27th, 2001

Dear Odysseus, bane of the Trojans,

I just returned from lunch with my publisher in the Trastevere. People say that the Trasteverini are the descendants of the actual Romans, being the most impassioned and violent of the modern denizens of the city. I would not argue with this as they seem to gesture as aggressively as the Neapolitans and other southern Italians. By the bye, I fell in love no less than four times during my walk about – it is not only the beauty of the Roman women, but how they carry themselves, so decidedly feminine, always impeccably dressed in black dresses, always painted in the finest makeup, always scented with what seems like a full-blooming bouquet of roses, and always ready for sensual pleasure that set them apart.

Compare this with American women who at times seem to be nigh impoverished, even if they possess the financial wherewithal of an heiress, wearing sweat pants, a baseball cap, and stinking of beer. A Roman woman would rather be crucified along the Via Appia than be forced to endure such barbarity! God, I love them, and I want to taste them all, every single one, even the 'brutta donnas,' simply to experience their elegance, their passion!

-Gabriele, child of Passion,

June 29th, 2001

Dear Odysseus, conqueror of Paris,

L'amour, c'est la lyre à sept cordes, et j'ai joué de toutes.

I have contracted syphilis from my excesses here, but I view it almost as a battle-wound, a manifestation of my many-pleasured conquests. I'm tempted to let it go untreated, perishing from its ravages. How poetic a death it would be to die of syphilis in Rome! In the very least, I would never have to leave Italia for America.

If I do happen to die from syphilis or anything else, I give you full legal right to my oeuvre on two conditions. The first is that you must burn my body in the classical manner, perched atop a pyre, a golden coin placed upon each eyelid as payment for the infernal ferryman Charon, with my flesh impeccably cleaned, oiled, and perfumed beforehand. The Persian 'attar of rose' imported from Persepolis is my personal preference, but I will defer to your refined judgment. Once my formerly beautiful flesh has been thoroughly burned, I would like my ashes spread throughout the various piazzas of Rome. The second condition is that upon my death you must hold ten days of games in Rome featuring the greatest poets, lyra players and athletes from Italia, Grecia, Magna Grecia, and beyond. If you fulfill these obligations then you, and you alone, have the indefinite rights to my oeuvre.

Speaking of oeuvres, I am making much progress on my satire, spending the evenings countering the revered Eliot, so idolized by the Anglo-American literati. God, they will despise me with such fervent ferocity, if they even deign to acknowledge my existence. I will send you some lines from my masterpiece in a few weeks when the work is more fully formed. I do think you will worship it, and me along with it, but then again I am a professed egotist, so of course, I would think this.

-Gabriele, the syphilitic Exile,

July 2nd, 2001

Dear Odysseus, of the wandering Soul,

Pasta and wine for breakfast, pasta and wine for lunch, pasta and wine for dinner. I am craving an American plate of meat and potatoes right now. I can hear you laughing all the way from Paris mumbling *'damned Yankee fool!'* to yourself over and over. But I do feel my muscles weakening, my body becoming as soft as a finely-feathered pillow. I cannot become as effete and effeminate as the men here. I must retain my 'manly courage' – andreia – and still be as 'kalos' as sculpted marble by one of the ancients. Remember, it was not the Roman army alone that humbled mighty Hannibal, but also the vast pleasures of pleasure-loving Capua. I am so exceedingly vain, Odysseus, but at least I admit my vanity whereas others go to extraordinary lengths to conceal or deny theirs, and surely there is some nobility in my admittance, eh?

Now, I must confess to you that there are certain elements of America that I do desperately miss: the sprawling gymnasias, the easy access to animal protein and fitness supplements, as well as the colossal supermarkets where one can find every conceivable food item imaginable. The last time that we spoke you were juggling three different Parisian fashion models while composing your novel. Has anything changed? Maybe one grew jealous and stabbed you slightly?

-Gabriele, the Supreme Scientist,

July 5th, 2001

Dear Odysseus Pane, man of Pain,

I am fearful that my publisher is involved with the Mafia. He has stated in the past that he owns some shares in olive groves in the suburbs surrounding Rome, which seems like nothing more than a front to me – didn't the Corleone family own Genco Olive Oil in *The Godfather*? Yesterday, we counted 120,000 lire in his studio, ostensibly for a business transaction. Do you not find it odd that a man would keep 120,000 lire in his apartment?

Well, the story becomes even more bizarre. During the following morning, I was sound asleep, dreaming of fair-tressed Calypso, when suddenly I was awoken by shouting. I heard a man screaming at my publisher who was simply trying to calm him down. I looked for a weapon, as the argument escalated to the point where I thought that the Italian might murder my publisher.

The only object that I could find was a pen, which I grabbed and began to walk towards the dining room. I thought about the famous query, *'Which is mightier, the pen or the sword?'* and Il Duce's response *'The sword, it cuts, ends things, finishes,'* which I thought to slightly revise with *'The pen, but only if it is wielded as a sword!'* So, as I approached the room, I was deliberating on whether I should stab him in the neck or the chest, finally deciding upon the neck. Mind you, all of these thoughts about the pen versus the sword, the location of the stab wound, and such, all occurred in the span of ten seconds or so.

But to my utter surprise, when I arrived in the room, my publisher and this man were now smiling and joking with each other. My publisher, Gianluca, cast a quizzical look in my direction, at a loss as to why I would be walking about half-naked, clutching a pen. *'Gabriele,'* he said, *'what on God's earth are you doing? Is this some sort of creative device that you use for inspiration, like dancing under the* moon?' 'No, no, sorry, I must have consumed too much wine last night, Gianluca. I apologize for the intrusion,' I mumbled before skulking back to my bedroom. As I walked away, I heard Gianluca say to the man, 'Poets! They're all mad!'

Though I was more the fool here – Don Quixote – than the hero – Achilles – you should know that I was prepared to fight to the death, half-naked, armed only with a pen!

-Don Quixote, son of Peleus and Thetis,

July 7th, 2001

Dear Odysseus, child of Beauty,

I wept today beneath the statue of Gaius Julius Caesar. He accomplished so much in his lifetime, and I am a complete and utter failure. I am nothing and nobody. At my age, Alexander was conquering the world, and what am I doing? Idling in Rome, writing poetry, and seducing the wives of the common bourgeoisie. I am a wastrel!

Yet, I do believe that some grand, herculean action could redeem me, and as such, Cyprus becomes more attractive. Even though I will probably be impaled and roasted alive, at least I will have done something with my life. I can only pray to the Gods that my fallen blood will fall upon the heart of a blossoming musk-rose, beautifying its spring-petals with the beauty and passion of my Grecian soul!

Literature teaches a man not only how to live well, but also how to die well. Here, I speak with specificity to strong-souled Patroclus, the Homeric hero, who chose to taunt full-glorious, full-beautiful Hector with his dying breath instead of pleading for his life like the gutless trembler, Lycaon. So Odysseus, what shall it be? Will you come to die with me among the strong-limbed Greeks, or have the tender-lipped sirens of Paris completely seduced your soul?

-Gabriele, of the Heroic Dreams,

July 9th, 2001

Dear Odysseus, man of many tongues,

By God, I do detest the vast majority of Italian-Americans visiting Rome and wish they would remain at the Jersey Shore, that bastion of egalitarian schlock, where they belong. I was walking through Piazza del Popolo dreaming of Cypriot glory when my dreams were interrupted by these 'barbaroi' with their overly coiffed hair, fake gold necklaces, and incomprehensible English. Besides all of these ghastly attributes, they reek of cheap cologne, while their women seem to revel in chewing gum with their mouths agape like a herd of grazing cows. These are people who think the actor Vinnie Pesca is somehow representative of Italy, instead of anything other than New Jersey.

Speaking on this subject, if you ever happen to be in America and wish to imagine that you are in Italia, you need not go to Mulberry Street, but rather to BellaFredos on Lincoln Road in Miami Beach. All of Lincoln Road, but especially BellaFredos, is an escape from the common trappings of Americana. Fashion models, heiresses, Arabian oil magnates, Argentinean trust funders, aesthetes, and artists populate its tables as international house music plays. One hears a bit of Italian, French, Spanish, Portuguese, and various other languages while lounging at this decadent venue. The average American from say Iowa or Minnesota would probably use the term 'Euro-trash' to describe its patrons. Yet, these 'ignorati' would be much better served to remain on Ocean Drive with the rest of the drunken tourists. Marcello Mastroianni would be at home here idling on this modern day Via Veneto, sipping espresso, surrounded by beautiful people. I remember one instance when a fair-formed feminine friend flew into Miami from Florence; she came directly from the airport to BellaFredos and exclaimed, *'Good God, Gabriele, I have not yet left Italy!'*

-Gabriele, The Prince of BellaFredos,

July 14th, 2001

Dear Odysseus, nemesis of Hector,

Today I was photographed in the manner of the last pagan God, Antinous. The photographer and I viewed numerous photographs of the Bithynian before making our selection. What a wonderful riposte to Courbet's quip, *'Show me an angel and I will paint one,'* a snarky aphorism expressing the sensibility of 19th century Realism. One needs only to replace the word 'angel' with 'God' before having Hermes, the guide and giant killer, deliver the photograph directly to Courbet in Hades. D.H. Lawrence understood my divine longing when he exclaimed, *'Give us Gods, Oh give them us! Give us Gods. We are so tired of men.'* I dream of what man can become, not just what man is, like the Italians of the High Renaissance.

This photograph truly illustrates the triumph of the imagination over mere reality. Though in this particular instance, I have translated my idealization of the human form, conceived in my imagination, into reality via vicious gymnasia sessions. For through my Napoleonic Will, I have transformed what normally would be considered Realism (the human body) into aesthetic idealism by attaining the physique of a heroic God: a man aspiring to be divine, as the ancient Hellenes once did. Oh Icarus! Oh Marsyas!

T.E. Hulme, the small-souled Prufrockian, profoundly misinterpreted the ancients when he incorrectly noted, *'In the classic it is always the light of ordinary day, never the light that never was on land or sea. It is always perfectly human and never exaggerated: man is always man and never a god.'* If only Mr. Hulme had read his Homer, the very foundation of 'the classic' more carefully, surely he would have noticed Homer's continual deployment of the adjective 'godlike' along with similes 'like a God,' 'handsome as a God,' and 'magnificent as a God' so often used to describe the high-hearted warriors. The boundary between men and Gods in 'the classic' is ambiguous at best, but if this Mr. Hulme wishes to remain a worm, let him be; that is his problem, not mine, Odysseus, for I will continue to dance upon the sun-kissed summit of Olympus with Dionysus, the wild-charging son of Zeus and Semele.

Many will view the photographic juxtaposition as megalomaniacal and hubristic, which it is, in one way, but alternatively it is designed to show the continuity of classical culture in modernity, in spite of (and *to spite*) the philistinism of the debased culture. I use the term philistine quite differently than the moderns who use the word to impugn those whom oppose the avant-garde: politicians from middle America, scolding moralists – be they clergy or not –, figurative artists, successful suburban bourgeois, and the like; whereas I utilize it to describe those whom unctuously bow before the mandated tenets of progressivity and transgressivity (an invented word), demanding that a work of art be 'original' and 'challenging' in order to be celebrated as opposed to aesthetic. The aesthetic has been banished into exile by the prevailing 'barbaroi,' yet I've always believed that whenever *To Kalon* is in decline, civilization is steadily descending into a state of barbarism, but fear not, my Parisian friend, as there are other rebels like us. Gabriela Lorca, Tadeusz Mickiewicz, Michele Lewberry, and the Classical Realists in NYC, immediately come to mind, for they are also defiantly and vociferously preaching the sacred gospel of beauty.

But enough of my digressive aside on my self-styled definition of the word 'philistine;' allow me to now return to the photograph in question. I brazenly assert that my body is as much an argument against modernity as my poetry. The moderns have told us that God is dead, beauty is dead, art is dead, but the only thing dead, Odysseus, are the souls of the men who pen such things. And I cannot think of a more appropriate counterpoint to their stance than this particular image: a bold declaration of immortal beauty! Though I am a wise fool and know that I know nothing at all – *To Kalon* – will never die, my friend; this much I do know.

-Gabriele, the brother of Antinous, the last gasp of Romanticism, the dying breath of Hellenism

July 18th, 2001

Dear Odysseus, ravager of soft-voiced nymphs,

This morning, a close friend revealed that a critic has hissed at my collection as *'tenth-rate Byronic gushings,'* to which I replied, *'better to be a tenth-rate Byronist than a first-rate Prufrockian,* trudging about the world 'measuring out one's life with coffee spoons,' wondering whether or not 'to disturb the universe.' Tell this sniveling worm, this scampering rat, this craven scarecrow, that not only do I disturb the universe, but that I am the universe!'

The critic went on to say *'Mr. Paterkallos, an arrogant ambitious nonentity, is a legend in his own mind, who suffers from delusions of grandeur, more in need of a psychiatrist than a foreign publisher.'* Of course I am a legend in my own mind, as all great men are merely legends in their own minds until society begrudgingly acknowledges their genius. Furthermore, if a man does not suffer from delusions of grandeur, I question *his* sanity, not mine, for it means that he has accepted his common lot in life, no longer dreaming of performing epic deeds. So, tell this Mr. Harrell, of the tweed bowties, that I proudly suffer from delusions of grandeur, but that with each passing day, my delusions of grandeur are steadily becoming a reality of grandeur, despite his best efforts!

I failed to ask, but I am certain that Mr. Harrell is American, English, Irish, Scottish, or something of the sort. They will never have me, nor I them, and let there be no peace between us. I do believe that the French, the Italians, the Greeks, the Arabs, the S. Americans (Latins) will recognize my genius, and that is enough for me. Speaking of the Latins, I love the fiery sensibility of their writers, whose books brim with blood, fire, and brimstone. Perhaps instead of a tranquil pen, they wield a stolen shaft of lightning when composing their flame-like lines.

How profoundly the Latin soul differs from the modern Anglo-American intellectual, a soulless scarecrow, who has two favorite hobbies. The first is to identify genuine emotion within an artistic work, proceeding to mock it with the hackneyed trope of the 'hallmark card,' while the second is to ridicule any manifestation of pure, idealized beauty in modernity (yes, beauty still does exist) as kitsch, demonstrating nothing more than their gross obeisance to the modernist mandarins. Bah humbug! Should I pull myself away from Goethe, Stendhal, and de Staël to challenge this man to a duel or to a gladiatorial contest? I could fight him as Dioxippus fought Coragus, completely naked, bathed in olive oil, covered in a lion head-dress, armed only with a club, standing before him as the incarnate God of War, Ares himself!

But let us now set this untermensch aside and ascend into beauty. Yesterday, I whiled away the afternoon in the Galleria Borghese, a veritable temple to *To Kalon* – it is filled with the most exquisite paintings and sculptures: Bernini, Canova, Titian, Raphael, Rubens, Caravaggio, and the like. My favorites are *Apollo and Daphne* and the *David*, both by Bernini. Bernini portrays the fleeing nymph in the very moment of transformation into a laurel tree to escape from the lecherous grasp of golden-bowed Apollo. Her marmorean tresses, translucent as polished glass, seem to be billowing in the blowing wind. She is so fully beautiful that I had an immense urge to rescue her from marauding Apollo, taking her as my personal concubine as Achilles took soft-belted Briseis.

What I love about the *David* is not only its technical mastery of the human form, but Bernini's choice to portray David as a masculine Grecian hero as opposed to a glyph – emaciated and androgynous (see Donatello's *David*), almost prefiguring the inevitable rise of the Galilean. Bernini's *David* is fit to be one of Leonidas' Three Hundred or a Macedonian following Alexander into the unknown depths of India!

-Gabriele, The Aesthete,

July 20th, 2001

Dear Odysseus, of the nimble feet,

Tonight the moon looks like a hammock of hammered gold brushed with ashen silver. Oh, for the Roman moon! Oh, for the silent furies palpitating within my wild soul! ***Sentio ergo sum. I feel therefore I am.*** It is in feeling, in sensation, that our existence is both confirmed and redeemed: the first gush of love, the flush of desire, the fire of passion.

Are you surprised by just how little Italian I've acquired on my Grand Tour? As you know, I am not a 'mingler' with the demos, partly due to my solitary disposition and partly due to my lame tongue. Is there any sight more risible than a man not only butchering the mellifluous Italian language, but stammering along as well? So, since the Gods have cursed me with this impediment, I must content myself with silence.

I spend most of my time reading in the English language: Homer, Neruda, Sappho, and the like. Even during my fitful fornicating fits there is very little conversation to be had, and any conversation had in those debauched moments is unfit for the contents of this letter. You will have to wait until we meet in person to hear all of the salacious little details of my harem-girls. I have been assembling the structure of the poetry collection, and have decided to open with 'Lie Down In My Poem,' which I view as one of the strongest in the entire collection and think that it will hold my name in posterity.

I'd like for you to lie down in my poem –
Sleep in the center of my verse,
And awaken on the tip of my quivering quill.
On days when you are absent, I am like impoverished gold or
rusted salt.
I am like austral ice that clings to its transient existence.
Can I melt upon your breast? Will you allow me?

I'd like for you to lie down in my poem.
Let flowers falling from your folding hair blossom in my lines.
Plant silver pears near my adjectives,
And allow your beauty to radiate like dashes of fire attacking
my running metaphors.

Will you bathe in the dew dripping from my syllables,
Or maybe bask in the light glowing from my ink?
Did you know that your primeval moans shape the shaky
structure of my poetic theorems,
And that the frozen topaz fleeing from your inner thigh
inspires my muse?

I'd like for you to lie down in my poem.
Rest your weary body upon my rough consonants.
Let your kisses trail my nouns like thirsty bloodhounds,
And in the white seas separating my spacious words, dive for
flourishing treasures;
Treasures lost by ancient Persian emperors.
Will you bear your chaste smile in my similes?
Please, my dear, don't let my verse become muddied with
despair.
Let it speak of heavenly smoke, dancing petals, beaming
grapes and loves that will not break.

So tonight, serenaded by the smooth voice of nightingales, fall
fast asleep in my poem.

-Gabriele, of the full beautiful poesia,

July 23rd, 2001

Odysseus, of the many epithets,

As I have told you previously, my publisher holds a very powerful position in the Vatican, and as such has arranged a private audience with the Pope. We were supposed to meet with him this morning, but we were bumped by the American President's impromptu appearance. Suddenly, ten SUVs stormed into the piazza like the war-chariots of Ares belched from the pits of Hades, with ominous dark-suited, dark-glassed men emerging.

I did not see the President, so maybe the Secret Service was properly securing the town for his impending arrival. So, instead of meeting with John Paul we explored Castel Gandolfo, a quaint little Italian town, rich in Romantic beauty. The prime attraction is the splendid view of Lake Albano that it affords; there is something so peaceful about sitting in a trattoria, sipping wine, nibbling on fresh bread, and simply luxuriating in the luxuriant view. I am so happy, so content here, that I could weep from the joys springing forth from my soul!

Before leaving the trattoria I sat for a long while, mesmerized by the Italian sun, a sun as regal as the adored eagle from the storied Roman standard: its rich rays resembled golden-painted petals sprung from a surreal daisy, or a series of burning sarissas bestride a well-burnished hoplon. Let others stand for the Galilean, for Reason, or for forced economic equality, but let it be known to all that I, me, Gabriele Paterkallos, stand for the furious passion of the Italian sun.

Your letters indicate that you are thoroughly enjoying your Parisian summer, reading and writing often, interspersed with soft-kisses from sun-kissed Parisian beauties. I am fairly certain that I would enjoy Paris, since the Parisians also share a love of The Beautiful, though I do think that I would miss the passionate mores of the Italians, but this is only conjecture on my part, since I will not know for sure until I make the 'odyssey' to Paris.

Will you share one of your women with me? I cannot go more than three or four days without the erotic attentions of the feminine race, for I start to develop migraines and various other ailments. She need not be as beautiful as one of your fashion models, but must be a little crazed and rabid.

-Gabriele, lover of Castel Gandolfo,

July 26th, 2001

Dear Odysseus, master of the dory,

Castel Gandolfo was indeed pleasant and charming, but I am now back in fiery Roma, the center of the world!

Oh Rome! My true home!
City of Eternal Beauty! Country of Immortal Poetry!
Oh, how I've missed you so terribly!

To recount my experience in Castel Gandolfo – I finally did have the opportunity to meet privately with the Pope, an invitation which I almost declined, since I was required to bow before him, an abominable action. I only consented since my Mother accompanied me, flying to Italy at the very last minute solely for the papal experience; for her, the meeting with him will rank among the most memorable moments of her life. So, out of love for my mother, and against my better judgment, I swallowed my immense pride and attended.

I did not crown myself in John Paul's presence *à la* Napoleon with Pope Pius VII, though I was very tempted to do so. Most people would feel grateful for having the opportunity to visit with the Pope, but after the ceremony, I was disgusted with myself. I had the intense urge to shower, to cleanse my soul from my obsequious, inglorious behavior. Will you forgive me for this, Odysseus? I swear on Zeus himself that I will never again bow before any man or God! And if I ever break this vow, I command you to summarily decapitate me for my proffering of 'earth and water.'

This morn, I visited Nero's infamous 'Domus Aurea' (Golden House). I read Suetonius along the way, laughing aloud at Nero's eccentricities. His philhellenism seems to be his only redeeming trait, as the man was a thorough monster, murdering nearly everyone in his purview. I adored the frescoes, as they reminded me of a painting by Tadeusz Mickiewicz, or one stolen from one of the

Pompeiian villas. As I walked about the Domus Aurea, I couldn't help but envision the Bacchanalias that must have occurred there – the clear-toned lyres, the Grecian dances, the writhing flesh. This domus is the very Eden of decadence. So, in honor of Nero, I corralled three nubile eastern European girls, whom I renamed Atthis, Anactoria, and Gongyla, dressing them in the Grecian manner by draping them in pure white sheets and garlanding them in wild-growing vines. Then, I had them, in complete unison, recite the choral ode from Euripides 'The Bacchae,' before devouring them as if I were Bacchus himself. I'm sure Nero, deep in fire-thrashed Hades, thrumming his lyre would have approved of my fleshy exploits.

This evening, just before my prurient excesses, I crossed paths with an American literary expatriate; though as a rule I generally try to avoid the literati as much as is possible, especially those of the Anglo-American variety. The conversation invariably turned to literature, with him gushing over Raymond Carver. I kept thinking to myself, *'What is Raymond Carver going to do for my soul?'* This man lives by his favorite expression, *'Things could always be worse – and sooner or later, they will be,'* the quintessence of cynicism, which he mumbles incessantly like a well-trained parrot. How profoundly his worldview differs from mine, as aptly expressed in the final lines of this particular poem of mine, *'In the distance – I hear a song – a simple song – a song of despair – a song of longing – and a song of sorrow./I have forgotten the words and the rhythm, but I sing./Yes, I sing.'* I am one of the few living artists who do not believe that pessimism is tantamount to wisdom.

But rather than engaging him about his trite pessimism or the merits of Raymond Carver, I just managed a half-hearted smile assuring him that I would certainly look into Mr. Carver. But I have to sincerely ask you, Odysseus: does this man really expect me to put down Pausanias, Virgil, and J.A. Symonds for Raymond Carver? An artist should hunger to discover rare colors in the midst of uncovering exotic flowers, aspiring to sing alongside Homer's golden-stringed lyre, a lyre sprung from the sweet-singing Castalian Spring. Promise me, Odysseus, that you will never submit to the philosophy of despair, especially since it is so passé and cliché in our modern day. Rather, devote yourself completely to the cultivation of ecstasy, knowledge, and beauty. And always demand more life! More life! More life!

But speaking on this American again, I kept wondering what on earth he was doing in beauteous Rome, and not in dispassionate New York, frigid London, or bohemian Berkeley where he belonged, where he could congregate with his type. And this brings me to my thought on art in general – would you not agree, Odysseus, that so much of art comes down to one's sensibility? Show me a man's heroes, and I will show you his soul, and if he has no heroes, you have revealed everything.

-Gabriele, the wild-eyed Dreamer,

August 1st, 2001

Dear Odysseus, Hero of Hellas,

I am in the midst of a 'young life crisis!' What will become of me, Odysseus? As you well know, it is unlikely that a man can support himself on poesia alone. Upon my return to America, and my graduation from university, I must find some type of employment. Yet, I have no talent other than bringing forth beauty into the world, other than singing, in concert and in harmony, with the songs of spring. And what will this bring me other than obscurity and poverty?

I would sooner die than work a menial job, unless I could secure a permanent sinecure. Maybe I should become an international criminal smuggling opium in order to support my art. Or maybe I should summon the courage to hurl myself from the summit of Castel Sant'angelo, or from the Leucadian cliffs as soon as my poetry collection is complete. Cyprus attracts me not only for the heroic death that it offers, but also as an escape from the 'quiet life of desperation' that surely awaits me.

-Gabriele, Nobody,

August 8th, 2001

Odysseus, the great tactician,

I am the wisest fool since Socrates! I had too much wine tonight and am writing to you for the sole purpose of announcing my divinity. **L'univers c'est moi !** I am beyond a poet, and am a force of nature, a stream of lava escaped from Vesuvius! Can you hear me pounding my chest all the way in Paris?

-Gabriele, a fleck of cooling magma,

August 10th, 2001

Odysseus, the Olympian,

While exploring the Jewish Ghetto this morning ribbons of rich matinal light were woven into the Italian horizon as if kissed by the silken threads of Artemis. My intention for this visit was simply to sample the renowned fried artichokes and other unique delicacies from this bohemian neighborhood, but, as always, Eros had other plans; a young maiden with lovely eyes cast her entrancing spell upon my soul, paralyzing me with her hypnotic beauty. She was loosely gowned and crowned in Asian-jasmine like a naiad from Arcadia now residing in Roma. She met my glance for a brief second, before turning away, disappearing into the balmy Roman day. Her eyes were the color of opal and amethyst locked in an eternal kiss. Oh, how I wished to dive into them, Odysseus, dying at the very moment that I possessed such divine beauty. I must return again sometime soon to hunt for this elusive goddess, for I am quite certain that the secrets of the universe lie hidden within her thighs.

I received two effusive letters in the mail today – the first from a young literary scholar in Berlin proclaiming that I am America's greatest living poet, and the second from a 19-year-old German girl named Eva. Eva is studying at one of the prestigious universities here in Rome; she informed me that she is writing a paper titled *'Aesthetic Poetry'* for her English class, and adverts to me within the essay. She asked if I would join her for an espresso in Piazza Navona to discuss her paper. I phoned her, and we agreed to meet this afternoon.

After reviewing her essay, which was actually quite impressive, we went back to her apartment, where I had my way with her, even taking her *'The Greek Way,'* which has nothing to do with Edith Hamilton. She was a proper virgin in this regard, but enjoyed it so that she asked if I would indulge in Act II tomorrow, so that she could revel in this newfound sensation. I too love *'The Greek Way,'* not only because I am Greek, but because it is so dominant and primal. It would have been fitting were I wearing a Viking helmet while *in flagrante delicto*, and perhaps I shall during our rendezvous tomorrow.

-Gabriele, The Barbarian,

August 11th, 2001

Dear Odysseus, skilled in combat,

Instead of going to Eva's apartment this morning, I went to 'Palestra Forte' on Viale Medaglie D'Oro to train my arms. I had a herculean training session with my muscles engorged to such an extreme degree that it seemed as if they were going to burst through my skin. Since the weather was warm, I decided to walk back to the apartment wearing just my stringer tank top and athletic shorts. After only a few moments on the street, I began receiving looks dripping with supercilious disdain; the same hauteur that I felt towards the Jersey Shore cast of characters was now directed at me by the glaring Romani.

I could almost read their minds: *'Put some clothes on. This isn't America.'* Though there were a few smiling young maidens and latent homosexuals (and some not so latent) who were appreciative of my fleshy procession. As I gently placed the key into the door, I pondered walking completely 'gymnos' during my next walkabout – garlanded in wild laurel – with my body bathed in a shimmering glow of olive oil to show the Romani my descent from antiquity.

I had a dream last night that perhaps you can shed some light upon. I was at Cape Sounion in Hellas, just a few feet in front of the Temple of Poseidon. I was completely naked save for stark white tape wrapped around my hands in the manner of a professional pugilist. There were two sea-nymphs by my side – one named Nafsica and the other Nesaea. Lovely-ankled Nafsica was dipping her delicate hand into a weathered amphora dripping glimmered honey, while white-armed Nesaea possessed a glittering amphora, worked in hammered gold by the hammer-smiths of Hephaestus, whose sheen reflected radiant shafts of Pierian light.

Nesaea's lustrous amphora gushed with golden olive-oil, flawless and fresh. Each sea-nymph covered their hands in their ambrosial liquid before rubbing it deep into my flesh in a slow, sensuous manner, as if to deliberately torture themselves with longing and desire, curable only by the fervor of the Sapphic lyre. Once they finished the task of anointing my body, they garlanded my brow with strands of stringed crocus, acanthus, and acacia, as if a stunning garden had suddenly sprung from my flowing locks – locks spiraling like a hyacinthine flower in a forgotten garden – part Antinouian, and part Jim Morrison.

The sea-nymphs then simultaneously kissed my cheek, and with a running leap hurled themselves into the cerulean majesty of the Aegean Sea. As soon as my goddesses abandoned me, completely naked and alone, my body covered in coveted honey and scented oil, I began to shadowbox furiously, as if I were sparring with the gallant sons of Achilles. After only a few moments, the sweat began intermingling amongst the oil and honey. As I sparred with my invisible opponents, the holy liquids now dripped down into the breast of the renowned earth, resting upon jagged rocks, coloring them in their bright brilliance. And as I continued on with my deft movements, movements as brash and brazen as the spear-thrusts of Hector, I looked as magnificent as a God.

After sparring for some time, the sparkling sun of Hellas began to descend into the wine-dark sea like a dense tangle of trained ivy vines climbing behind a trellis. The sky was the color of wild mauve, pale violet, and lurid lavender lavishly spun together on a virginal palette by a dexterous artisan, creating a new color heretofore unseen by mere mortals; this was presently the surreal hue of the sky, my friend. I so wish you had been present in the dream with me, so as to see the chromatic-scheme of the dreamy horizon as it kissed the beauty-kissed sea. I now ceased sparring so as to enjoy the entwining light clashing in kaleidoscopic conflagrations of color. I stood there – alone – enraptured by the enchanting beauty of Nature.

Just as the sun became exactly halved, achieving a kind of harmonious 'symmetria,' I saw an armada of blackened ships lurching over the horizon like a collocation of tiny sticks – my utopian scene had been graffitied by reality. As they came a bit closer, I could discern the Turkish crescent, as if the singular sun had been usurped by innumerable invading moons. The Turks had sent ten thousand of their finest vessels against Hellas, and there was but one option: to meet these ships by my lonesome if necessary. So, I emulated the sprint of my sleek-haired, smooth-armed sea-nymphs, leaping into the Aegean Sea with hopes to swim directly towards the enemy, fighting with my bare hands or perhaps borrowing the sea-hewn trident of Triton sinking as many ships as possible before The Barbarians speared me like some ungovernable sea-monster rabid for blood and destruction.

Yet, as I hurtled towards the wayward Aegean Sea in a vertiginous free-fall like a drunken dreidel given wooden wings, I realized that I did not account for the rugged rocks assembled upon the seashore like an armed infantry arrayed in a sinister meadow, a meadow absent flowers and maidens, endowed only with death-dealing daggers, medieval pikes, and rapacious sabers. I glanced downward once again – glimpsing these pointed tips of earth glaring back at me as if I were fast approaching the bowels of Hades. And just before I was impaled by these earth-borne lances, I awoke in a cold sweat.

How do you interpret this dream, Odysseus? For me, it is obvious – it is a warning from the Gods advising us to abandon the war in Cyprus; they have foretold of our failure, refusing to grant us victory over our enemies. This revelation, however, will not deter me in the least. For a man's destiny is not written in stone, but in water.

-Gabriele, Destiny,

August 12th, 2001

Dear Odysseus, great-souled,

 Today I met with Gianluca's printer. I inquired about using my own blood instead of ink to print the first copy, but this idea was vetoed by both Gianluca and the printer. I think you will be impressed with the tome, since much care is going into its aesthetic look. We are including photography and artwork vis-à-vis the poetry, which will enhance its visual appeal. Additionally, we are using the highest quality paper available, as the very paper of a book should give one's fingers immense pleasure, not only delighting one's soul, but one's senses as well.

 Eva has been telephoning me incessantly begging for her 'Greek teacher,' to give her a tough lesson, but I have been too consumed in Tacitus this afternoon to venture to her boudoir. Maybe later on this evening, however, I will summon the energy to ravage her properly. In your last letter you mentioned your plan to travel to Provence with Fanny for a week. I do hope that you two had a pleasurable time, and I look forward to hearing about your tales from the jaunt.

 Most recently at a dinner party, I was introduced to an Athenian-born economist who teaches at one of the Universities here in Rome. I had hoped to ask him about Cyprus, to see if he could link me with other fighters, but I couldn't get a word in edgewise, as the man droned on and on about the evils of the forthcoming EU currency, prophesizing that it would be catastrophic for the Greek economy. I don't know anything about economics, my friend, so I just listened quietly, nodding my head here and there – and drifting off occasionally into fantasies of Cypriot glory, for the dreams of my soul are much more interesting than the tedium of the external world. For me, dearest Odysseus, the external world exists only as a 'thing' to be conquered or renounced, and I so often oscillate between the two.

-Mr. Paterkallos, professor of economics,

August 13th, 2001

Dear Odysseus, of the lustrous tunic,

I am in the midst of composing a speech that I will deliver to my assembled troops in Cyprus. Here is what I have thus far:

Heroes of Hellas! Children of Zeus!

It is presently only six words, but is it not a glorious six words? I kid. I kid. Here is the speech. Instead of reading it silently to yourself on the paper, throw open your window, and deliver it passionately, replete with wild hand-gestures to the passersby on the street below.

Heroes of Hellas! Children of Zeus! It is a true honor to lead you into battle against The Barbarians. Your presence here indicates that you are more than willing to make the ultimate sacrifice on behalf of the ideal of freedom. No value is dearer to the Greek soul than freedom, not even beauty. However, if you are one who loves life more than honor, leave now – this campaign is not for you. For 27 years the Turkish army has been garrisoned comfortably in Cyprus, unmolested, unchallenged, while our Grecian brethren have twirled their worry beads and danced in tavernas like a harem of drunken women on opium, as if nothing were seriously amiss.

Our politicians have negotiated ad nauseam at international peace-summits, while the Turkish soldier has continued to walk freely in Nicosia, Famagusta, and Kyrenia. These days are over. Let our enemy now look over his shoulder; let him suffer through sleepless nights, not wondering if the forces of Hellas will strike, but when and where.

No one [dramatic pause here] save you men assembled here has had the audacity, the courage, and the will to oppose the Turkish military presence in Grecian lands. This is how I propose that we now negotiate with our enemy. [At this point in the speech, I will hurl a spear east in the direction of our enemy; however, I would not advise you to do this from your balcony in Paris as you are delivering this speech to the pigeons on your windowsill and the random tourists walking by.]

It is through the blood of heroes, not the similes of poets, the golden-tongued speeches of orators, or the petitions of well-intentioned activists that freedom is attained. Freedom is only earned through the eloquence of action, and oftentimes violent action. I promise you that in the depths of Hades, Leonidas and his 300, Kolokotronis, Diakos, Grivas, and other far-famed heroes are watching our every movement with rapt admiration. Surely, Byron and Feraios are composing feverish poetry to Sappho's lovely lyre so as to inspire us to achieve immortal deeds on the battlefield.

Not only are we being watched by these great men of the past, but by Greece itself. While many of our peers in Athens are shrouding their faces in the manner of Persian Immortals and protesting against the conglomerate of foreign bankers at various G8 conferences by hurling Molotov cocktails, we stand here defiantly, defending the very honor of Greece. Our actions shame them, and many others who have chosen to remain neutral. I swear to you, my heroes, that in the years to come their flagrant inaction will haunt them like some ghoulish albatross hung about their necks perpetually feasting upon their intestines.

It has been prophesized by the oracles that I am to fall here in this struggle; when this news was recently relayed to me, I could only smile since I consider it to be the highest honor to die amongst you, the bravest men of Hellas. Perhaps it is the will of Zeus that we all are to fall here, defeated and destroyed to a man; perhaps we are simply here to inspire the generation after us, or if that generation is too cowardly, then perhaps two generations hence.

One cannot control these things; however, one can control how one fights. And I beseech you in the most ardent way, from the very core of my being, that when the enemy is in sight to fight like an army of wild beasts suffering from starvation whose very existence depends solely on the success of the hunt. Let the Turkish soldier exclaim in frustration to their commanders, 'We are not fighting an army of Grecian men, but an army of Grecian Gods!' Through your bold deeds, your lives will come to be defined by your actions here. If in your past, you have proven to be a trembler, a coward, one who shirks from the fight, yet here in Nicosia, in this epochal struggle, you manage to summon the courage of a hero, you will forever be remembered as a hero, and a hero only.

And I promise you, as Zeus is my witness, if we fight well, our mutual sacrifice will stand as a deathless monument to freedom, to Hellenism. Not only Greece, but the entire West will remember us with fondness, for fighting for justice against sheer force. And when we finally descend into Hades, we will be welcomed by other high-hearted heroes, truly fit to stand in their presence. They will say, 'Here are the 300 heroes of Cyprus who stood against 30,000 well-armed, well-trained barbarians. Come, my friends, have a drink with us, and tell us of your heroic exploits.'

I will end with the words of the hero, Harmocydes, culled from the pages of our immortal ancestor, Herodotus:

'Now, then, is the time for you all to show yourselves brave men. It is better to die fighting, and defending our lives, than tamely to allow them to slay us in this shameful fashion. Let them learn that they are barbarians, and that the men whose death they have plotted are Greeks!' Nicosia or Death!

-Gabriele, of the Heroic Dreams,

August 14th, 2001

Dear Odysseus, seducer of wayward nymphs,

I was going to write a poem titled *'Ode To Joy,'* but then I realized that there was no need to, since life itself here in Rome is pure joy, pure poetry. *Isn't it far better to live a poetic life than to spend one's life writing poetry?* And speaking of poesia, I went to the Keats-Shelley House located in Piazza Di Spagna today. Keats died there from consumption at 25, just 4 years older than me.

I left a lock of my hair and a sheaf of my poetry as a tribute to him. I would have liked to leave a few droplets of my diseased blood, but I probably would have been imprisoned for such an overwrought display of affection. When he expired, he assumed himself to be a failure, as he could barely give away his books of poetry, with his own publisher glumly noting, *'the world cares nothing for him.'* Keats' soul was as beautiful as one of the ancient Greeks, and hopefully it now wanders in Arcadia strumming a lyre, plaited in gilded laurel, singing his nights away with the nightingales. One can only hope for poetic justice such as this. Josiah Conder, an anti-Romantic of the age, (shall we call him the father of T.E. Hulme?) impugned Keats' timeless 'Ode on a Grecian Urn' by saying:

'Beauty is truth, truth beauty,' – that is all
Ye know on earth, and all ye need to know'

That is, all that Mr. Keats knows or cares to know. – But till
he knows much more than this, he will never write verse fit to
live.'

And no, this wasn't published in last month's *London Criterion,* but in a predecessor of theirs, *The Eclectic Review* in 1820. I only joke here as I am a great admirer of *The London Criterion* for standing against the 'nihilistic absurdities' and the 'dadaist pathologies' perpetrated in the Art World today. I know that they will never have me though, as I am much too Romantic a personage for their Neo-Modernist longings (I would not dare insult them by saying, Post-Modernist). Anyways, enough of my digression here, let us return to Mr. Conder. Surely, Mr. Conder now languishes alone in Hades, with the other souls mocking him thusly: *'This is the worm who criticized beauty-loving John Keats.'*

-Gabriele, The Romantic,

August 15th, 2001

Dear Odysseus, defender of the Greeks,

I boxed for a long while today, a new hobby of mine. I believe that it was Diogenes of Sinope who astutely noted that *'A man should be something of a God, a woman something of a flower,'* and for me, it is now imperative to not only look like Achilles, but to fight like him, as well. The Greeks advised balance in all things, my friend, so I must spend less time in The Gymnasia and more in The Palaestra. I am not very good at boxing, to be very honest, but if I apply myself over the next few years, I may become fairly decent.

For example, I was not blessed with a strong body, but through the sheer force of my indomitable Will, I have become something of a living God, worthy of Antinous and Alcibiades. I use the phrasing 'something of' to slightly mitigate the egotism of the statement, though knowing you as I do, I'm sure that you would have preferred that I say, 'I have become a living God,' deleting the expression 'something of,' no? You are giggling like a schoolboy right now, I'm sure.

After I finished boxing, I returned to the apartment to read the excerpts from your Novel. I love it! You must continue onward until they award you the Nobel Prize in Literature with the ceremony held upon the peaks of Parnassus, and you crowned in the manner of Corinne! I only ask that you do not forget about your obscure poet-friend, pitying my poverty in some way when society finally acknowledges your genius.

I am having an urge to escape Rome, which has become a den of iniquity for me, longing to travel into Magna Grecia – Naples, Paestum, Pompeii, Herculaneum, Positano, and even Sicily. Goethe famously said, *'To have seen Italy without having seen Sicily is not to have seen Italy at all, for Sicily is the clue to everything.'* As you well know, I am inclined to take Goethe at his word, and feel that it is imperative for my soul to somehow reach Sicily, the golden garden of the Mediterranean.

-Young Gabriele, son of Werther,

August 17th, 2001

Dear Odysseus, of the diamantine prose,

A most disagreeable morning! Do you remember the American literatus whom I had the displeasure of meeting a few weeks ago, who had the temerity to recommend Raymond Carver to me? Well, somehow this little weasel got a hold of my manuscript and had the impudence to drop off his 'notes' for me. Can you imagine the audacity of this peasant? He is not worthy to stand in the shadow of my shadow, and yet he offers his 'notes.'

This time I did not bite my tongue, and told him explicitly, *'If you have so much as altered a single mark of punctuation in my manuscript, I will cut you!'* before slamming the door. What can one expect, as he is a product of the American MFA system, a system, that by and large, views literary creation as a collective act instead of an individual one; there are exceptions to this, of course, but this is the prevailing orthodoxy, as they sit around in kumbaya circles critiquing each other's work. May Zeus save me from these people!

I am demanding that you read Winston Halprin's 'A Hero from The Great War,' which is a modern masterpiece, and who very well may be 'The Last Romantic' besides us, of course. His genius is immortal, though it is doubtful that he will garner many literary awards since his politics are center-right, and he is somewhat of a mercurial figure. I do think in the end ('the end' being posthumously) that his genius will triumph over the horn-rimmed-spectacle-wearing PoMo mandarins in control of these things.

How can these small-souled nihilists understand the Homeric soul of Halprin? Sometimes I venture into the Villa Borghese to read his work for hours on end, re-reading many passages simply for their verbal beauty. There is a vignette about the flight of swallows on page 430 that might just be one of the most beautifully wrought passages in all of western literature. And the denouement of the novel moves my soul to such a degree that I cannot gaze upon it more than once a month. If I ever have the opportunity to meet Mr. Halprin, I would place my hand upon his chest, so that the beauty of his classical soul would transfer into mine via osmosis.

But it is past time to set aside the beauty of literature for the beauty of Nature. I am now off to bow before the torrid Roman moon, Odysseus; a moon that has risen into a state of surreal madness, for folds of emeralds are emblazoned into its snowy crest, emeralds that glimmer like an ancient Arabian necklace draped upon ivory flesh. Shall I howl at its comely breast like a wild-souled wolf?

-Gabriele, of the tumultuous Passions,

August 21st, 2001

Dear Odysseus, teller of tall tales,

It has just come to my attention from my friends in America that my completely nude 'Crombie and Lauren' photograph depicting me climbing into a helicopter is creating quite a scandal with many Christian groups encouraging a boycott of the clothing retailer. My particular photograph is being paraded about by the Galileans as one of the prime offenders. The LA Times writer Rachel Steinem just released a column about it, along with sundry other American newspapers. I am completely indifferent to what the hoi polloi and the Galileans think of the photograph, and in a way court their disapprobation.

Their common sensibility led to the destruction of many illustrious Greek and Roman sculptures, when the cult of the Jewish carpenter was firmly entrenching its tyrannous stranglehold upon Western civilization; they viewed the glories of antiquity as idolatrous, and therefore dangerous. I swear to you Odysseus that if I had a time machine, I would return to rescue Hypatia from Cyril's henchmen, disemboweling the lot of them, before dying in front of the wondrous sculptures, resisting the Christian barbarians to the last breath. What a glorious death! My heroic blood spilt upon the fallen Pentelic marble of the classical Masters!

Having said this, and knowing your sensibility as I do, I am certain that you will approve of the photograph's immortal beauty. The ancient Greeks would certainly have celebrated it, since they were true devotees of beauty, and probably would have created a cult in my honor. I emulated the Romantic countenance of Alexander in the famous mosaic where frightful Darius reaches towards him.

Though I am merely ascending into a helicopter, I look as if I am stepping upon the hallowed summit of Olympus. Speaking on this, another friend indicated that it is possible to hike to the pinnacle of Olympus, a feat that we must accomplish sometime soon. I will try to assemble the best lyra players of Crete to accompany us so that when we reach the crest, we can have a Bacchanalia replete with Homeric readings and Dionysian music!

-Gabriele, of the Dionysian dances,

August 22nd, 2001

Dear Odysseus, conqueror of Arcadian naiads,

I am sitting alone on the balcony writing to you, just delighting in the Roman moonlight. The polished moon, in its full-flown glory tonight, looks like a well-crafted discus hurled from Olympus. Its colorful hue, vivid and vivacious, is casting a silvery blue spell upon the polis: enveloping eternal Rome in its empyrean palette.

I have received your letter and am happy to hear that you are dressing as Napoleon and walking about the streets of Paris. Maybe some of the tourists will bow at your feet. Speaking of Napoleon, have you read his love letters to his Josephine? You should read them in their entirety, but here is one just to give you a sense of their unbridled pathos.

I am going to bed with my heart full of your adorable Image...I cannot wait to give you proofs of my ardent Love... How happy I would be if I could assist you at your undressing, the little firm white breast, the adorable face, The hair tied up in a scarf à la creole. You know that I will never forget the little visits, you know, the little black forest... I kiss it a thousand times and wait impatiently for the moment I will be in it. To live within Josephine is to live in the Elysian fields. Kisses on your mouth, your eyes, your breast, everywhere, everywhere.

If Napoleon so desired, he could have renounced his quest as a conqueror and undoubtedly become the Neruda of the 18th century. We should do the inverse, abjuring literature to become European conquerors. I've already conquered the women of Rome, so I am fairly certain that we would have tremendous success. Would you desire the capital in the East or the West of our empire?

My satire is coming along nicely, focusing solely on the T.S. Eliot section thus far. I am still not yet ready to show you vignettes, but I assure you that it will be a masterpiece. A friend advised me to focus on the literary lemmings, Bukowski and Ginsberg, leaving Eliot be, since without the Eliot section, I would receive the approval of many highbrow professors, neo-formalists, and conservatives. But if I savage Eliot, the purse-lipped Pope of

High Modernism, he informed me that I will have no allies, no admirers, and will stand completely alone. I told him that I am well aware of this, but that I prefer to stand alone at Thermopylae, with only Beauty and Truth serving as my guide, rather than engage in artistic appeasement.

Surely, it would be less controversial to take his advice, but I must oppose Eliot's *'Great No!'* for the *'Great Yes!'* of Romanticism! I can admire Eliot's lifelong devotion to *The Logos*, but cannot countenance his dreary world-view, for as you always say, *'These are heroic times!'* I will continue to sing of heroes until my lyre is set ablaze by the Turks! Every night now I dream of a Grecian triumph in Nicosia and ask Zeus himself for his blessing. *If Alexander could have the known world, can I not have a single isle?*

-Gabriele, Man of Dreams,

August 24th, 2001

Odysseus, the man of many ways,

This morning I was walking into Piazza del Campidoglio designed by the immortal, Michelangelo, when suddenly it began to rain. I looked up towards the sky, a sky the color of stained purple velvet, and thought for a moment that I could discern the profile of Hera in one of the darkened clouds. Surely, she had unexpectedly returned to Mount Ida, finding lascivious Zeus arrayed with one of his mortal lovers, and in her despairing rage burst into a flood of tears.

As I sprinted for some kind of cover, I espied a cortege of priests. Now, as you know Odysseus, many modern intellectuals despise the clergy – accusing them of being predators, pedophiles, and the like, perpetually hurling superlative aspersions at them. Yet, I do not detest these priests in the least; rather I *envy* them for their unwavering faith. Oh Odysseus, if only I could believe as these men do!

I am now in the apartment drinking wine and reading Baudelaire's magnum opus – *Flowers of Evil* – a work that could easily be renamed '*Kalon Kakon.*' Eva informed me yesterday that her girlfriends at the university have hung my Crombie image on their wall and are so enamored with my nude body that four of them have already agreed to host a saturnalia in my honor within the next few days. Should I betray my Hellenic soul, dressing myself as a sultan with my four concubine girls?

Four may seem impressive, but you must remember that the God – Marc Antony – kept 100 in his personal harem. If I do indulge, I will scent their taut youthful bodies in the finest Persian perfumes of Persepolis, while covering their flesh in the fairest olive oil in all of Italia, before interweaving rose petals into their finely-dressed tresses. My God, the debauchery! Please burn this letter after reading it, so that it does not fall into the wrong hands.

-Gaius Gabriele Paterkallos, the proprietor of The Golden House,

August 26th, 2001

Odysseus, of the well-limned prose,

As you well know, I have often sneered at those who self-publish, but it seems a viable alternative in order to retain total control over one's work. My publisher has chosen an ill-suited cover image for *The Soul of A Young Man*. He is adamant in his selection and will have none of my protestations. Never again allow me to mock those who self-publish as amateurs. Sorry for this short epistle, but I hear a faint strain of the lyra, and my soul yearns to dance under the gypsy moon, so I must go immediately! Aman! Aman!

-Gabriele, lover of Eleuthera,

August 27th, 2001

Dearest Odysseus, of the Parisian Parties,

Though we are very similar in many ways, we are also different in others. You delight in the balls and galas of society, while I would rather suffer the evening in a Turkish prison than endure one of these festive fêtes. Whenever I am forced to attend a social event, I feel as if my skin has been dipped into bubbling lava, as if a thousand vipers are feasting upon my intestines, as if a school of malnourished piranhas have established temporary residence upon my arteries. I think of nothing save a furtive escape back into my solitude.

Surely, I must suffer from some form of social anxiety disorder, and I would hope that if I were to come to Paris, you would not compel me to appear at one of these events that you so often frequent. While you are the gypsy, Odysseus, wandering about the world, I am Achilles, the melancholic loner, thrumming my lyre in my tent, singing songs of brave heroes and of my longing for long-tressed Briseis. I am content to while away my time in Phthia until there is some grand, epochal action to pull me away from the pleasures of The Athenaeum, The Lyra, and The Gymnasia.

Additionally, you seem enthralled with the Mycenaean Greeks, but have little to no regard for the high classical era and thereafter, whereas I am interested in the continuity of Hellenism, in the peripheries, the lacunae, so often ignored. Modern Hellenism interests me as much as classical Hellenism – Cavafy as much as Archilochus – Diakos as much as Diomedes. You are probably unfamiliar with Diakos, who is no less a hero than Diomedes, and after reading of his glorious death, a death that we moderns can only dream of, you will be forced to concede this point to me.

Diakos, a bold leader of the Greek Revolution against the barbarian Ottomans, decided to halt the Ottoman advance by taking a defensive position in Thermopylae. Yes, my friend, *that* Thermopylae! As you can see, the soul of Leonidas was alive and well in the 19th century! After suffering heavy losses at Alamana Bridge, he was encouraged to retreat by his comrade, Bousgos, essentially saving him and his men for another day, but Diakos refused, remaining with 48 hardened warriors to resist the Ottomans for as long as they were able.

After fighting for many hours in ferocious hand to hand combat, he was finally captured and taken before Omer Vryonis, the Ottoman commander, who was so impressed with Diakos' military acumen and manly courage that he offered to make him an officer in the Ottoman army, if only Diakos converted from Christianity to Islam. Diakos refused uttering the now famous phrase – *'Ego Graikos yennithika, Graikos the na pethano'* – *'I was born a Greek, I shall die a Greek.'* He was subsequently impaled and roasted alive, and whose final words are the very soul of poesia. *'Look at the time Charon chose to take me, now that the branches are flowering, and the earth sends forth grass.'*

Only a Greek, or in the least one with a Grecian soul, would comment upon the beauty of spring just moments before being tortured in a most barbarous manner. Surely, Mr. Pane, you must admit this man, and admit that he is no less of a hero than any of the Homeric Greeks that we unabashedly worship. Diakos' death so inspired me that I have recently composed this poem about him, which contains 19 exclamation marks, far too few a number for renowned Diakos; it must have at least 25 before it is finished!!!!!!

Oh Diakos!
How I wish I was with you in Roumeli!
Fighting next to the blossoming cypress tree
Bleeding profusely,
so that one day Greece may be free!

Oh, Olympian Divinities!
Please, let me be one of the great 48!
Destined for a truly heroic Fate!
Defending Liberty against Tyranny,
while fulfilling a Homeric Destiny!

Oh Diakos!
Let us resist the invidious invaders
like our ancestors of yesteryear
who fought like Lions, absent any fear –
Like Spartans clashing with The Barbarians!
Protecting these hallowed lands
from the clutches of Persian hands.
Like the Cretans against the Germans,
Or like a klepht or a brave palikari,
slaying the mighty Ottomans!

Oh Diakos!
I wish to garland you in sprigs of spring-basil
Bushels of laurel
And wreathes of fennel!

Honoring your glorious story with my sword of swinging fire,
With my wondrous words soaring into Pierian wings,
And with the starry singing of my glistening lyre.

Oh Diakos!
I wish to bleed on the very spot where you so gloriously fell!
Where the blood of high-hearted Heroes
waters these breezy meadows –
Planting indomitable boughs – boughs of Freedom!
Look at the time Charon chose to take me
Now that the branches are flowering
And the earth sends forth grass.

Oh Diakos!
You are the equal of Immortal Leonidas,
The very spirit of Hellas!
But where does your bold soul now sleep?
Are you with Androutsos in Gravia?
Or in Missolonghi with Nikitaras?
Yet some say that you weep
upon the slavish streets of Nicosia –
Dreaming of the colossal battle of Alamana –
Hoping for just one more last stand,
fighting to the very last man!

Oh Diakos, I wish to die with you once again,
my fearless friend,
even if it's just the two of us
versus the best of men
from Northern Cyprus!'

-Gabriele, son of Diakos,

August 28th, 2001

Odysseus Nymphegetes,

To answer your question – No, I am not working on a novel, though I know that I probably should, since novels are more marketable than poesia. But I have no intention of 'tumbling down into prose,' content merely to wear the rich roses of poesy, reveling in my relative poverty, wanting nothing, needing nothing, expecting nothing.

Speaking of 'nothing,' I recently had a tattoo placed upon my hip, though as a general rule I despise tattoos, finding them barbarous and crass, but in a fit of spontaneous hypocrisy, I opted to have the phrase *'Aut Caesar Aut Nihil,'* the adopted maxim of Cesare Borgia, permanently inscribed upon me; the English translation is *'Either Caesar or Nothing.'* When I first obtained it, I dreamt of becoming 'Caesar,' but with each passing day, I long to become 'Nihil,' but not a Nihilist. I now wish to renounce society, not conquer it, nor even reform it.

I simply desire the luxury of privacy and leisure time, so that I can live a Greek life – spending half of the day amongst my books, studying *The Logos*, being a student of philosophy, of literature, of The Beautiful – with the remainder of the day devoted to the body: weight-training, boxing, and wrestling. The divine Wilde informed us that the Greeks gave us two types – the artist and the athlete – why must I choose only one?

-Gabriele, descendant of Pindar *and* Dioxippus

August 29th, 2001

Dear Odysseus, illustrious Ithacan,

I am writing to you at 4:34 am, as I have been awoken by a tremendous dream! Morpheus revealed my first action as supreme commander of the Hellenes in the Cypriot campaign, but before I address that, I must give you some historical perspective, so that the revelation makes sense to you. In 1996 Petros Petropolomou (what a poetic name!), a Greek Cypriot, was killed by Turkish armed forces while attempting to climb a flagpole to remove the Turkish flag; he has become a hero-martyr in both Greece and Cyprus. After the incident, the Turkish Prime Minister condoned the murder of Petropolomou, and further threatened to sever the hands of anyone who insults their flag. So now, we can return to winged Morpheus who spoke to me in these dreamy words.

'Gabriele, child of Hellas, you must use the words of The Barbarians to your advantage, taking bold action so that your enemies think you to be completely mad. Let them come to dismiss you as a vainglorious fool. Take this knife and give the sons of Mehmet a gift of your finger along with this attached epistle.'

'It has come to my attention that you have threatened to sever the hands of those who insult your flag. Enclosed you will find a personal gift that I wish to bestow upon you, a head-start if you will: a soiled Turkish flag along with the tip of my pinky finger. Should you desire to finish the task at hand, you must come into the battlefields of Nicosia to do so. And you should know that my Greeks and I will never surrender, so the only path of victory for you is to slay us to a man, which I am sure would give you immense pleasure. Molon Labe barbaroi!'

Somewhere in Hades, Achilles and his Myrmidons are smiling. I would not be surprised if the young palikari of Hellas emulate me, sending the tips of their severed pinky fingers to the Turks! Hah! Can you imagine 10,000 pinky fingers arriving at the Turkish embassy? *The madness! The glory!*

I still have not yet decided on the location for our training camp, but I am thinking that it should be based in Thermopylae, Marathon, Plataea, or Olympia before we walk upon The Mediterranean Sea making our way to Cyprus, of Aphrodite's maiden dance. I will consult with the Delphic oracle very soon to determine the most favorable polis for our training, but I am personally leaning towards Thermopylae or Olympia. Picture the faces of random tourists on holiday chancing upon 300 nude men preparing for battle! Anyways, enough of my madness for tonight; please burn this letter immediately upon reading it, for obvious reasons. I will leave you with a few lines on the hero-martyr Petropolomou:

Oh Petros Petropolomou!
We have not forgotten you
For you have taught us the value
of manly virtue.
And someday soon, phile mou,
We shall avenge you!

-Gabriele, of the 9.5 fingers,

P.S. My second action as commander involves a finely-wrought wooden horse, but I will reveal the details to you in another letter, as Hypnos is beginning to rest upon my aching eyelids.

September 1st, 2001

Dear Odysseus, swayer of men's minds,

Since my training sessions have fallen off a bit here in Rome, I have begun dabbling in anabolic steroids. Were you to reveal this to your learned Parisian friends they would likely dismiss me as a 'monosyllabic troglodyte' for this habit, but for me, the use of these supplements is to transcend humanity, to become Nietzsche's 'Overman,' overcoming 'the real' for 'the ideal.' I am presently taking testosterone, anavar, winstrol, and human growth hormone, and have already been able to add a few pounds of muscle.

The man from whom I purchased the products inquired whether I would be willing to sell it through his connections in America upon my return. It is highly dangerous, but could be quite lucrative, and if I were able to avoid apprehension by the police, it would allow me the leisure time that I so crave. I must consider the matter more deeply, but in the very least, you must promise me that if I were to become imprisoned, you would send me beautiful books to pass the time.

Now, let us leave the gallows for the poetic peaks of Mt. Helicon where the sweet-voiced muses sleep soundly upon the resounding bow of flowing-haired Apollo – where the nymphs and the naiads dance gently under the swaying oak tree – and where Artemis is savagely kissed by pleasure-kissed Bacchus. Please read the previous sentence aloud so as to revel in its aural majesty.

The literature of the 21st century will be free of the shackles of the previous century and will be aesthetic, heroic, Romantic, classic, and classical. You and I are the harbingers of this change, my brother, but it will probably only occur after our deaths, so we will be forced to endure an execrable, exiguous existence ignored and relegated to the literary ghetto, but no matter, we will still be gazing upon the Pleiades: hungering for more experience, more sensation, more beauty. We are not merely men of the times, Odysseus, *but men for all times!*

-Gabriele, idolater of the Pleiades,

September 3rd, 2001

Dear Odysseus, wanderer on the wine-dark sea,

In America, one must be something, but in Italy, one can simply be. Do you understand this distinction? In America, one must constantly be scurrying about like a wounded rat on amphetamines trying to acquire as many ducats as one is able by becoming a dedicated careerist. Being hurried and harried is the norm. One does not exist outside of one's realm of employment; it is truly defining, but in Italy, the supreme goal is to feel alive, to drink the ambrosial nectar of life, so a job is merely an accessory, a necessary evil, if you will. While the Americans lionize Wall Street tycoons (Horatio Alger types), gladiators, errr, athletes, and actors, the Italians correctly canonize scholars and artists.

And to this exact point, many of my peers from The Harrowford School have chosen to doggedly pursue the rank acquisition of gold, while I have chosen a vastly different path, a path rarely taken. I have elected to hunt for the rarefied principle of beauty. And I have contemplated beauty for so long and with such ardent intensity that my soul has become a golden butterfly.

In America I have to almost apologize for being a poet, being greeted with such vulgar questions as, *'How many books have you sold?' 'Can you make any money from that?'* whereas here I am regarded as a gift from the Olympians. Now, do not misconstrue my comments and label me a Marxist, which I am certainly not; it's just that I have no real ambition in the hoarding of gold. I desire just enough to sustain myself, just enough to escape the work-a-day reality of the rabble. Leisure time is my true aim, for it is only in sustained periods of leisure that a man can attain his *Areté*.

Now, reverting back to the topic of Communism, I've always considered it a misguided strain of Romanticism. What could be more Romantic than the notion of shared resources and wealth within a society? Unlike the rabid free-market adherents and the cultists of Ayn Rand who bow before the cracked altar of Reason, I do not view Marx as a diabolical antichrist, but instead see him as a Romantic personage, expressing the dreamy idealism of his soul like a Goethe or Chateaubriand. While other artists have chosen paint, marble, or language as their desired medium, Marx's canvas was mankind itself, an impossible proposition, which only further enhances his position as an arch-Romantic.

One must surely note however that the forced application of an idealized theoretical construct upon the world of men is destined for failure. Man is not as malleable as ink. Communism presumes the perfectibility of man, not taking into account the tenets of greed, envy, ambition, love, lust, and the like. Plato himself learned this cruel lesson in Syracuse while trying to implement his 'Republic.'

Society has witnessed the utter horror of Communism in action and should now know that it is best left to the pages of Romantic philosophy or to the drunken musings of the Symposium – certainly, not a system to ever be considered again for actual implementation. Democracy can be messy, inefficient, and frustrating at times, but it is without question the finest system of government the world has yet seen. American democracy, even with all its faults and foibles, still remains the school of civilization. And if a future society decides to ignore my sage advice here, they need only to read Golding's *Lord of the Flies* to see how their tale will end.

-Gabriele, The American Athenian,

September 5th, 2001

Dear Odysseus, Ithakan Hero,

Do you not find it highly ironic that my publisher is well-placed in the Vatican? I am an unquestionable apostate with my poems being hymns to paganism, well, one should say Hellenism, but that is another matter for another letter. Gianluca informed me that the Pope enjoyed my book, most especially the short story. Thank God he misinterpreted it, for if he had read it properly he may have encouraged my publisher to abandon the entire tome.

I do not think that you have read my Nietzschean allegory about The Defiant One, but it ends with God punishing him and his followers by summarily destroying them after they refuse submission. One should regard them as doomed heroes with The Defiant One representing the ideal of freedom. You, being the Nietzschean that you are will appreciate the short story, I think, so I will include it with this letter.

I am very disappointed in The American Cultural Institute in Rome. I had thought that they would position themselves as an oasis of aestheticism, a sanctuary of beauty in modernity, but they have succumbed to the sophistry of The Age, longing to appear contemporary (one may as well just say 'temporary'), avant-garde (what a disgusting little word!), and progressive (or more accurately 'ugly'). They patronize novelists who write 'firmly in the moment,' and 'painters' who possess an undying admiration for Marcel Duchamp.

One would assume that they would hunger to discover the next Winckelmann, but alas my friend, I think they dream of supporting the 21st century Greenberg, a man most famous for his ridiculous maxim, *'All profoundly original artwork looks ugly at first.'* The strict adherence to this horrid phrase has helped bring about the decline of beauty in modernity with his anti-aesthetic acolytes blindly chasing the tenet of originality as opposed to the principle of beauty. Don't you feel, Odysseus, that it is much nobler to pursue beauty instead of progressivity? I cannot imagine the ancient Athenians exclaiming, *'How original! How ugly!'* at the public unveiling of the Parthenon Frieze.

After pondering this tragedy for some time, I turned on the lyra music of Diomedes Dramantis, and quietly wept to myself for the decline of τό καλόν, and the fall of Greece itself, which are really one and the same. Perhaps I can help bring about a renaissance of Hellenism in modernity. I so value our budding friendship, Odysseus, since without you I would be completely alone in this vast wasteland, surrounded by 'barbaroi,' like Ovid in Tomis amongst the Scythians. Though we are ignored by the universities, the cultural institutions, the mandarins, and the general public alike, one day we will triumph!

-Gabriele, the castoff,

September 12th, 2001

Dear Odysseus, of the great war-cry,

Those motherfucking cocksucking cowardly sons of bitches! Can you believe this? I was glued to the television all day yesterday. I have often been critical of American cultural mores, but not the ideal of America, for She carries the mantle of Western civilization, born so long ago in illustrious Athens.

America may have made foreign policy errors in the past, but I've always believed that Her intentions were *and* are noble. The castrati on the Left wish to 'understand' why we are hated by the Islamic world, even to opaquely assert that we deserved this response. How soft we have become! *'Quinctilius Varus, give me back my Legions!'*

We should hit those sons of bitches so hard that their ancestors in Hades cough blood for centuries to come, and this includes their false prophet, Mohammed! I trust no culture or religion that demands its flock to bow five times daily like some common slave. Such barbarous slavishness is anathema to one with a Grecian soul like my own. The American Left can view me as a fascist, a jingoist, a warmonger, or whatever they'd like, but these eunuchs have no heart, no andreia! These are people who live by the pacific cliché, *'An eye for an eye leaves the whole world blind.'* Well, I say, better to be blind as Homer, yet free as an Athenian, than be a clear-seeing slave. And it was the celebrated Chian, Homer himself, who noted, *'For Zeus of the wide brows takes away half a man's worth once the day of slavery closes upon him.'*

Were you able to view the coverage in Paris? I cringed every time that I saw a body falling from one of the Towers. Hopefully the individuals were already deceased, because I cannot imagine the sheer terror in one's soul as one soared through the sky like some accursed bird without wings. Maybe I should put Cyprus on hold and volunteer for the American Military, requesting the most dangerous missions available.

-Gabriele, defender of Western civilization,

September 13th, 2001

Dear Odysseus, glory of Achaea,

Sometimes a man needs to reject Reason, a limited entity, turning instead to the silvery splendor of the silent moon. Oh Odysseus, how I adore the brightly-lit moon, which tonight looks like a sharpened saber dangling from the waist of a wandering corsair. Oh, to be lost in the reveries of the autumnal moon, to be rescued by the astral state of anoesis!

I am spending a few days in Montepulciano, a charming little Tuscan town. The slow cadence of Tuscany is a welcome change from the frenzied, frenetic pace of Roman life. I've been walking alone throughout the countryside, steeped in profound melancholy, but inordinately happy, which are not antipodes, in the least; there is something pleasurable, one could even say, beautiful, in melancholia. Weeping alone under the Tuscan moon is one of life's wondrous joys!

I feel that in Italy I've finally found a culture that I can be a part of instead of one that I am constantly opposing. I do fear that when I return to America, I will become embittered and curmudgeonly, losing the soul of John Keats, becoming as bilious as Mencken. Isn't it so much more sublime to be *for* something, rather than *against* something? It is exceptionally tiresome, even debilitating, to be perpetually spitting into the wind – one is much better off dancing under the Tuscan sun.

I've been reading Petrarch and Dante often during my Tuscan retreat, but have also begun reading a historical novel set in Thermopylae titled *'The Hot Gates'* written by Stephen Poesianne. As you can imagine, I adore it, escaping daily from 2001 AD back into 480 BC picturing myself engaged in training for hours on end preparing for the inevitable arrival of the Persian hordes.

My publisher and various other friends have encouraged me to pursue acting in order to take advantage of my physical beauty, but I have no real interest, partly due to my introverted nature, and partly due to my lame tongue. I can already hear the cackling of the grips and the production assistants as they mock my stammering speech. Furthermore, I am a child of passion, not a fool of fame, much preferring my anonymity, at least for the time being. Truthfully, I do not possess the passion for acting like I do for the written word. It would just be a pursuit with the intended aim of extracting as much gold from society as I could, so as to retreat back into my cave. I would much prefer to be an extra in *'The Hot Gates'* should it ever be turned into a film than be the star of a contemporary film.

In fact, I would give Poesianne and the director full legal rights to kill me during the climactic battle scene. If I cannot return to Thermopylae proper, this would be the closest alternative. And hopefully there wouldn't be a filming malfunction during the very moment when I was impaled by one of Xerxes' Immortals.

-Gabriele, The Spartan,

September 14th, 2001

Dear Odysseus, breaker of Troy,

I certainly do not regret my decision to take a semester off from university so as to spend a bit more time here in Italy, and am cherishing every single moment. As you say in your previous letter to me, *'Time cannot be spent. It only can be squandered,'* and I intend to suck the marrow from every second of my life. I will probably be able to remain here another month or so before being forced to return to America.

Speaking of America, I recently received a letter from a highly talented 31-year-old poet living in Boca Raton, Florida. It is a delightful letter, so I shall share both its contents and my response with you, but I must say before I proceed that it is very strange for a poet to choose to live in Boca Raton, of all places!

> *Dear Mr. Paterkallos,*
>
> *My good friend Bella introduced me to your poetry, which I thoroughly enjoyed, especially your grecian themed poems. I have published two chapbooks of poetry thus far, and was wondering if you could give me some advice regarding the publication racket as well as the writing process in general. I have also included a few of my poems for your perusal. Bella informed me that you live in Miami, which is only an hour's drive for me, so maybe when you return to America, we could get together. Thank you!*
>
> *Fondly,*
>
> *Richard Joya*

Here is my response.

Dear Mr. Joya,

The poems that you sent me are very beautiful, so it does not surprise me that you remain an obscure figure in American Letters, since the culture that we presently live in is disinterested, if not hostile, towards beauty. If it means anything to you, should we ever meet, I will personally crown you in Grecian laurel for your rarefied artistic sensibility. Though the world has no use for you, know that I, me, Gabriele Paterkallos am a fervid admirer of your poesia.

The only genuine advice that I can offer you in regard to writing is to cultivate a beautiful soul – become an ardent student of The Beautiful in all of its diverse and wondrous forms. For me, the creation of poetry is not an aim unto itself, but rather, the petals blossoming from this noble endeavor. In fact, I am always a moment away from renouncing literature entirely to become a common gardener in Arcady.

The pursuit of beauty is reward enough, so even if one should 'fail' (however that is to be defined and determined is anyone's guess), one can in the very least remain a custodian of The Beautiful, a conserver of tradition. Society has had enough of the deconstructionists and is in dire need of constructionists – the nature of your work clearly demonstrates that you are of the latter rather than the former. I wish you well, and should I ever return to America, it would be my pleasure to meet with you.

Your Admirer,
Gabriele Paterkallos

I neglected to include the following advice in the letter to Mr. Joya, so I will relay it to you instead: one must endeavor to emulate the detached stance of a tenured university professor towards commercial sales, writing with blithe indifference to such common concerns, having no interest in pandering to the masses. Now, if the previous correspondence and my pretentious addendum were too literary for your tastes, Odysseus, here is a letter much more emotional and profligate.

Dearest Gabriele,

A poem of yours was read aloud in our book club last week. I must confess that I could actually feel my heart palpitating faster and faster with each succeeding line read, and by the end of the poem my entire body was flushed, my brow and various other areas of my body damp. I cannot recall the last time that I had such a visceral reaction to modern literature. You have awoken passions within my soul that have been dormant for many years, and I am immensely grateful to you for this. Once the host concluded the reading, she displayed a picture of you, and I nearly fainted.

Surely, this is not you, but a fraud modeled on the tale of Cyrano de Bergerac, perpetrated by your publisher to sell copies of the book. I must see you in the flesh myself to satisfy my gnawing curiosity. If you consent to this, I shall be idling by the Colosseum at 2 am next Saturday evening. Should you arrive as Gabriele, and not Cyrano, both my heart and my flesh are yours to do with as you see fit. I have included a recent photograph, a few drops of my blood, a lock of my hair, and a six line poem with this letter. I trust that you will burn this letter upon finishing it in the name of decorum and discretion.

Are my feelings real or just my imagination?
When the thought of you takes me to a place of deep sensations.
Is it wiser to be a fantasy?
Since the real is often so brief, like a fire burning in heat.
Today I hold my heart carefully so that my beats don't get heard
And I treasure the moment that you came into my world.

Forever yours,
Contessa Alessandra da Vinci

Life is grand and glorious, and I wish to live forever amongst my fawning odalisques! I will certainly be at the Colosseum next Saturday evening to meet my new admirer, Ms. Alessandra. Hopefully I can ravage her in the bowels of the Colosseum itself like an ancient gladiator intent on having his last fill of pleasure before stepping into the Arena to face certain death!

-Gabriele, the debauched Gladiator,

September 16th, 2001

Dear Odysseus, son of Laertes and Anticlea,

I am utterly exhausted today and can barely move since I spent four to five hours last evening ravaging every inch of Alessandra's body. My chest, arms and especially my inner thighs are bruised with bite marks, and will probably be for some time; some of the blood that this succubus extracted, as if she were part-Arcadian-nymph and part-vampire, even stained her ottoman divan imported all the way from Istanbul. *How poetic!*

Hopefully it is an omen from the Gods regarding the future liberation of Cyprus from The Barbarians. Perhaps someday soon my blood will be shed in the pursuit of liberty, instead of lust! Her husband was away in Croatia on business, so we had the entire palazzo to ourselves, and even had the audacity to involve one of the live-in servant girls in our erotic shenanigans.

I plan on doing absolutely nothing for the rest of the day, except curling up with my books in total and complete solitude. If I go more than a day without the ability to retreat back into my isolation, I become as miserable as a teething babe denied a nap. Besides writing to you, I've also been corresponding with a former teacher of mine, Edward Haverwell, from The Harrowford School, in Harrowford, Pennsylvania. He is the first man to truly take an interest in the development of my mind: discussing literature and philosophy with me for hours on end in his classroom and at various dinners. My time with him remains some of the most cherished moments of my short existence. Oh, how I miss Edward, and think of him every day!

One final matter before I go – you asked in your previous letter as to why I continue to say 'poesia' as opposed to 'poetry,' and the answer is not simply because I am presently in Italia. I feel that if one says 'poesia' as opposed to 'poetry,' one is more inclined to compose in the manner of Algernon Charles Swinburne; whereas, if one says the Anglo 'poetry,' perhaps one will become Jeffrey Hillen, the heir to Eliot and Pound, and I can think of no worse fate for a poet, except perhaps being confined in a room where Bukowski is blared on a perpetual loop! Ha! I'm losing my mind, my friend! You must come to Italia soon, so we can pursue many-pleasured adventures.

-Gabriele, Don Jooan,

September 18th, 2001

Dear Odysseus, man of too many epithets,

I was in a fight last night and came out on the losing end of it. I was walking on the Via Margutta on my way to dinner when I came upon an Italian couple in a heated argument, an argument that escalated as I approached, with the man raising his hand as if to strike the woman. I, of course, tried to play The Hero, but the man hit me with a three punch combination, knocking me to my knees, whereupon he delivered two devastating kicks to my chest. I was informed this morning that the man who bested me is the far-renowned Italian kick-boxer, nicknamed Fredo.

I am okay, but will probably need a week or so to recover with no gymnasia sessions, which is a kind of death for me. I will go mad with boredom, although I will take advantage of the time by reading more, and allowing my tender-eyed sultanas to tend to my wounds. I am somewhat depressed as you can imagine. How am I to liberate Cyprus from The Barbarians if I cannot even win a common street fight?

On another note, membership into the Byron Society was extended to me, but I am much too Byronic a personage to be part of any society that would have me, even the Byron society, for I am an island unto myself.

-Don Quixote

September 20th, 2001

Dear Odysseus, pride of the Argives,

What a complete rogue I am! Alessandra's husband came to the apartment this afternoon with two well-built Romanian ruffians. I was in Piazza del Popolo nursing my wounded pride, but thankfully my publisher informed them that I had returned to America and would not be back to Italy for some time. This disappointed them obviously, as they were intent on extracting an ounce of blood for every minute of pleasure given to his wife. As you can imagine, based upon my proclivities, it would have been a prolonged and bloody affair. I often have these Romantic notions of a heroic death, Odysseus, but I fear that I may someday die in infamy at the hands of a cuckolded husband like this Count da Vinci.

I heard from a mutual friend that the matter is a complete disaster, somewhere between a farce and a tragicomedy. Apparently, Alessandra came home earlier than expected and found her husband 'occupied' with the same maid whom we coerced into our pleasures, though based upon this anecdote, she apparently needs little coaxing. Anyhow, Alessandra went into a rage, screaming loudly, and even assaulting her husband and the maid; in the ensuing melee, the maid divulged Alessandra's indiscretions, and her part in them. Alessandra has been put out of the house, returning ignominiously to her familial estate, somewhere on the outskirts of Rome.

My God, what have I done, Odysseus? I am cursed by the Gods, for anything that I touch eventually falls into some sort of ruin. How could I have resisted her insistent letters though? A man is a man, so if a lovely-armed young woman throws herself at my feet, how exactly am I supposed to respond?

-Gabriele, the fallen angel

September 22nd, 2001

Dear Odysseus, father of Telemachus,

The Alessandra matter continues on unabated! Just this morning, a messenger delivered this to my publisher's offices.

Dearest Gabriele,

I am in exile at my parent's estate in Tivoli, doing nothing but reading your poetry under the moonlight and dreaming of your touch. Why have you not written to me? I could live on just one beautiful line for a year! Just one line! For me! Though you seem to have no use for my kisses and valentines, I shall continue to send them forever and ever! I shall throw myself at your feet, like the humble slave that I am – enslaved by your masculine beauty! How I long to worship you. . . at your feet. . . to kneel. . .

Will you not come to rescue me from this base existence with your towering kisses? We could leave this all behind, running off to Paris, Moscow or Leros! Please hurry, Gabriele, for every day that passes without you, another dagger pierces my fragile heart, a heart which is now yours – please come to claim it, I beg you! I have enclosed another lock of my hair with this letter.

Forever and ever yours,

Alessandra

God damn!

Has she gone mad? (And with all of this hair accumulating from my admirers, I could open a wig making business!)

Does she not know that I have no prospects – no job, no sinecure, no trust fund? I am presently so impecunious that I am seriously contemplating becoming a dealer of narcotics, and am so emotionally unstable that I am always a moment away from opening my veins so as to escape my impoverished future. How am I to respond to such a letter as this? I think silence, though inordinately cruel, is the only option.

Speaking of narcotics, the man here in Rome from whom I've been purchasing the anabolic steroids mentioned that his friends in Florida are launching a company called YouthMedicale, and they have offered me a sales position upon my return to America. Essentially, there is a loophole in the law enabling them to sell human growth hormone, and steroids as an 'anti-aging medicine,' with a doctor rubber stamping the prescription; it seems a grey area legally, but could be very prosperous for me.

What other prospects do I have, my friend? Shall I endure savage poverty, while trying to compose beautiful poesia, or should I become a proper villain, a pariah of society? Though on further thought, I probably should just submit to the advice of my family, sit for my LSATS, and live a life of wealthy obscurity.

-Gabriele, the villainous heart-breaker,

September 24th, 2001

Dear Odysseus, long enduring,

I spent the last few days in the environs of Tivoli – visiting Hadrian's villa and my inamorata, Alessandra. Hadrian's contemporaries referred to him as 'Graeculus' (little Greek) for his love of all things Greek, including young

Greek boys, as evinced by his worship of the beautiful Antinous. Walking through the villa is a pleasurable little excursion, not as pleasurable as pillaging Alessandra's flesh, but pleasurable nonetheless.

I am officially done with Alessandra, however. Though she is a great provider of pleasure, she longs to possess me entirely, and nothing is as off-putting as a clingy woman. She dreams of keeping me in Tivoli as her captive, playing the role of Dido to my Aeneas. Upon saying our goodbyes she would barely release me from her grasp. I must throw myself into Roman life for as long as I am able, procuring new pleasures, new sensations, before making my inevitable return to Philistine.

On the way to Tivoli, I passed a red Lamborghini, which I must admit is a very impressive automobile; however, I've never had the urge to possess such an ostentatious vehicle. Rather, I've always dreamt of owning a high-hearted stallion, the color of the Calabrian night. I would ride him throughout the streets of Rome, which of course would send the moderns into apoplectic fits. There is something inordinately divine about viewing a horse in full-stride, its lithe muscles fully flexed with every movement.

I will name my horse Xanthus (the horse of Achilles), with plans to ride him into battle against The Barbarians. Let them have their clumsy tanks, while Xanthus's swift, nimble hooves evade them like a circling bee taunting a frustrated house-cat. I will ride between these mechanized beasts like some avenging God, hurling grenades until only a cemetery of twisted metal remains. Aman! Aman!

Speaking of horses, I will also finally reveal to you, and to you alone, how the conflict will commence. I will have the greatest craftsmen in Hellas, the sons of Hephaestus himself, construct a monumental wooden horse, towering above both man and machine. The most skilled painters in the greater Greek world will adorn the horse with painted depictions of The Barbarian heroes – Mehmet II, Genghis Khan, Attila The Hun, and Ataturk – wheeling it to the Green Line in Nicosia as a gift from Gabriele and his Greeks. After this action is filmed and distributed to the numerous media outlets for maximum exposure, the horse will be detonated: a symbolic first act in our war. Ah, how poetic! You must burn this letter, Odysseus, so that it does not fall into the tawdry hands of Turkish agents. Long live Hellas!

You will probably protest that the West will not support my war against the Turks, even intervening against me. I cannot bring myself to believe this to be so. My enemies are descended from Genghis and Attila, blood-thirsty tyrants, going so far as to flaunt their barbarous ancestry by naming their invasion of Cyprus as 'Operation Attila.' Let my campaign be termed 'Operation Plato' 'Operation Leonidas' or perhaps 'Operation Freedom.'

Though it pains me to admit, upon further introspection, I think that the West would back the Turks, not from any firm ideological bent per se, but from sheer political opportunism. Despite its atrocious record on human rights, the West views Turkey as one of the 'moderate' voices in the Islamic world, while the Greeks are mired in poverty, regarded as a burden. But though publicly the Americans and others in the West would support the Turks, I do believe that deep in their souls, they would silently support my struggle in the 'Land of Heroes,' longing for the announcement to ring out: *The Greeks have liberated Nicosia! The Greeks have liberated Nicosia!'*

-Gabriele, the sane madman,

September 26th, 2001

Dear Odysseus, pride of Ithaka,

After contemplating the sentiments expressed in my previous letter, it suddenly occurred to me that I did not account for the very real possibility that the Greek government would send its own professional military to disband my private army. Do you think that they would have the audacity to oppose me? I do not believe they would dare such a thing! Surely, their soldiers would defect, with their men comprehending that it is better to die fighting The Barbarian than other Greeks, especially Greeks devoted to defending the glory and honor of immortal Hellas. No race of men, Odysseus, has longed for heroism more than the Greek, and what could possibly be more heroic in modernity than fighting the illegal Turkish occupation of holy Cyprus? But just to be circumspect, I will inscribe the poem below on the path into Nicosia for the eyes of the heroic-eyed Hellenic warriors.

'Fellow Greeks, Sons of Zeus,
I implore you to join us
in our noble struggle for freedom
from The Barbarian
in Cyprus.

But if you are unable to perform this task
then I would only ask
that you fight poorly against us
against men who have sworn to defend the True and the Just.'

So, what do you think, Odysseus? Will the Greek government attempt to quash my rogue army of heroes, or will they allow us to pursue liberty and glory?

Let me now transition from the battlefield into the gymnasia. How impressed you would be with my new body. The steroids are really working. I now weigh 210 lbs! Soon, I will no longer merely be a demi-God, but a proper Olympian. My well-muscled body has attracted all sorts of admirers especially the young 'donnas' here in Rome. I've sampled six different ones in the last twenty-four hours and am thoroughly exhausted. The most dangerous liaison was with Flavia, the towel-girl from the gymnasia, who yanked me into a back room so as to 'worship' my body. *Oh, the Pleasure! The Pleasure!*

I have accepted the position with YouthMedicale. I will work as much as I am able to during the few years left of university, sending them 'patients,' at my convenience, and possibly assuming a full time position upon my graduation. I know that you are probably disappointed with this decision, but my financial anxiety grows daily. I am planning on returning to Miami sometime soon for a long weekend to meet with the owners and to view the construction of the compounding pharmacy.

You do not have such plebeian concerns, since you receive a monthly distribution of $2,000 from your trust fund. While this does not give you an extraordinary amount of wealth, it gives you just enough of a cushion to renounce society, giving yourself completely to literature. How I envy you for this, my friend! I do not have such a luxury, and must find some way to support myself. So, please do not be cross with me regarding this choice of mine.

-Gabriele, the reluctant bourgeois,

September 28th, 2001

Dear Odysseus, tamer of horses,

Yesterday, I had a photo-shoot with the fêted fashion photographer, Christopher Hakkos. He keeps a studio here in Rome along with his primary one in Philistia (Manhattan). He paid me $3,000 to pose for a coffee table book that he is working on, which will include some of the most beautiful men in the world. Oh, to be young and beautiful! Do you realize how many books I can buy with this money? I'm estimating about 150 to 200 just from the two hours of 'work.'

I'm writing to you right now from Piazza Navona, quite possibly the most gorgeous of all Roman piazzas. I'm sipping espresso while listening to two bedraggled gypsies sing Puccini's 'Vogliatemi Bene' gloriously; the poverty of their dress belies the richness of their souls. Several years ago, a young woman named Psyche told me that butterflies fly through our souls, yet I had not fully believed her, until now. When I hear a song such as this, a song possessing such transformative beauty, I am convinced that mankind is partly divine, or in the very least divinely created. Though we spend much of our existence grunting along for survival, there are unique moments, moments inscribed with ineffable beauty, when one is briefly transported to the heavens, moments when one is reminded of our purer nature, of our immortal soul. Beauty is tantamount to divinity.

But now, let me move on from my platonic musings, so as to sketch my surroundings for you. To my left is a French couple who are devouring each other with fiery kisses, while on my right a family from Chicago is so appalled by the prurient display that they seem to be on the verge of complaining to the proprietors. I purposely avoid eye contact with everyone here, so as not to get pulled into a superficial conversation. I prefer to be alone, but alone amongst the demos, for is there anything more terrifying than actual solitude?

Have you ever danced a Zeibekiko, Odysseus? It is a dithyrambic dance with no formal steps – one's feet are led by one's soul. The dance has its roots in ancient tragedy, but it is still very popular in modern Hellas; the Zeibekiko is an expression of self, as if the dancer is communicating to the audience 'this is who I am.' When it is danced properly, a man can shed his humanity, becoming divine, if only just for a brief moment. Wild leaps followed by guttural yawps, and Dionysian gestures are part of the alluring Zeibekiko.

If I come to Paris, we will wait until the argentine moon lined with tufts of polished ivory ascends into its full-flowering fullness, before going into the streets to dance a glorious Zeibekiko. We will bring a wide-rimmed amphora filled with crumpled paper and napkins that we will set aflame just before we begin our dance! Under the burning, burnished moon, brimming with passion, we will circle about the fire with our arms outstretched like two proud eagles in full-flight destined for Olympian heights. And every so often we will pour ouzo upon the flourishing flames nourishing them with this liquid ambrosia. Ah, I can already envision it, my friend! Aman! Aman!

-Gabriele, The Zeibekiko Dancer,

September 29th, 2001

Dear Odysseus, Parisian flâneur,

It's a good thing that my soul is beautiful, because my body becomes more diseased with each passing moment. I was diagnosed with 'the clap' this morning. What can I expect for suffering from the excesses of passion? I indulge every single sensual urge that passes through my soul – giving full reign to my body's erotic cravings. I may live a short life, Odysseus, but it will be filled with more pleasure than the lives of one hundred common men.

I probably contracted this new affliction of the flesh during my most recent *ménage à quatre*, which, by the bye, are more trouble than they are worth. Trying to satisfy three women simultaneously is more stressful than pleasurable, with invariable jealousies erupting when one caters to one nymph over the other. Do you have the same issue during your *ménages à quatre*? So, henceforth, I renounce the *ménage à quatre* and will only partake in the traditional *ménage à trois*.

Yet, how I tire of sensual pleasure and long to do something heroic! What will become of me? Will I eventually be a 40-year-old rake chasing after 20-year-old Swiss girls here in Rome on holiday? What kind of lowly existence is this? I know that I repeat this lament to you often, but this thought torments me daily. In fact, I have added these few lines into my burgeoning satire.

I have swum in harems of fair-haired women
Immersing myself in the Excesses of Sin
And I can tell you with utter certainty
That there is no Epiphany found in Depravity
For Dissolution only breeds Disillusion.

This afternoon, after reading Homer, I closed my eyes and gave myself completely to my dreams. For dreams, as you know Odysseus, are the very lifeblood of existence. I imagined the undying fame to be attained in the Cypriot campaign – either to cede or seize glory!

-Gabriele, The diseased Epicurean,

September 30th, 2001

Dear Odysseus, slayer of Agelaus,

I seem to get as much attention, if not more, from gay men as I do from women. I think this springs from my physical beauty coupled with my interest in Art; they just simply assume that I am of their persuasion. I've always tried to be gentle, yet firm in my rebukes, and seem to be at a loss as to how proceed. If I vociferously assert my heterosexuality, they will say 'thou doth protest too much,' and if I say little, it will be interpreted as a tacit admission. So, what is one to do, Odysseus? I am trapped between Scylla and Charybdis.

Mind you, I bear no ill will towards homosexuals, as some of my greatest intellectual instructors have been of this proclivity. In fact, during my campaign against The Turks I plan to resurrect The Theban Sacred Band, an elite regiment of 150 male couples, who humbled proud Sparta at Leuctra in 371 BC before falling to a man against Alexander in Chaeronea in 338 BC. I think they will be some of my bravest warriors, and while we are on this topic, I must say that I truly don't understand the American military policy of banning homosexuals from their ranks (disguised under the name 'don't ask, don't tell'), for if the Americans only had a sense of history, they would realize that these men would be an asset, not a detriment. But, what can one do, as their government is strongly influenced by southern evangelicals. Did you notice the Freudian slip in the last sentence? I said 'their government' as opposed to the proper 'my government.' Can you not see that I am becoming a thorough exile?

Now, let us go from the topic of homosexuality to that of heterosexuality. I think many of my women sleep with me not only for my physical prowess, but also to satisfy their own vanity; they know my reputation as a libertine, and they falsely assume that through their influence, and their influence alone, they can redeem me, tame me – reforming me into a monogamous angel. Yet, they all fail, of course, with many leaving embarrassed and embittered. Everyone loves a challenge until they fail at the challenge, no? My heart has been wounded more times than I care to remember, so if I am destined for failure in love, can I not at least be a fantastic success in the pursuit of pleasure? What else is one to do?

Here is a little anecdote that will make you smile. Yesterday, when I arrived at a café in Piazza Navona, I noticed a famous American film actor seated to my left. But as soon as I walked in in my black pinstriped suit all of the women ceased fawning over him, directing their lusty attention towards me. I could see his countenance immediately change becoming colored with indignant confusion. I could almost read his mind: *'Who the fuck is this? And why are these women paying more attention to him? Don't they know who I am?'*

Though he has more gold than Croesus, and I am nigh indigent, I stole the scene from him. I must go now, as I have a dark-eyed, dark-skinned beauty staring over my shoulder wondering why I am writing to you instead of presently devouring her, and now I am wondering the same thing, so I bid you adieu, as I descend (or should I say 'ascend') into sensual pleasure.

-Gabriele, part-celebrity, part-sensualist, part-littérateur, but wholly nothing,

October 1st, 2001

Dear Odysseus, smooth-tongued,

There are few things that give me more pleasure than walking alone under the Roman moonlight. I do think that I am the most melancholy man in the entire world, but also the happiest! I can sit for hours on end in an abandoned piazza simply gazing upon the rosy-fingered moon as she hurls similes seething with ancient ardor into my soul. Sometimes, I have the urge to become a savage wolf, getting on all fours, howling loudly at its crystalline crescent. Do you think me mad for such thoughts? Tonight the moon is shaped like the flag of The Barbarians, yet one can still slightly discern its shaded body, as if it were veiled in an empurpled veil, perhaps the very one that once mighty Agamemnon strode upon, upon his ill-fated return to Mycenae, rich in gold.

Last evening, I spent the entire night – alone – wandering about the streets of Rome lost in my dreams until finally after many aimless hours, the rose-robed-dawn with her rosy light blossomed upon the Roman horizon. I opened my mouth so as to drink in the grandeur of the melting sun, hoping that its radiant light would purify my soul. And so after worshipping both the moon and the sun, I was thoroughly exhausted, intent on simply returning to the apartment for some much needed sleep, but I chanced upon one of my many Italian inamoratas who kindly invited me to her palazzo to rest, but as you can imagine, we did not end up sleeping. I performed quite badly since I was exceedingly fatigued, craving the comforts of sleep more than the pleasures of the flesh, but the experience was still pleasurable, nonetheless.

-Gabriele, The Egotist,

October 2nd, 2001

Dear Odysseus, lover of Trojan women,

Today I spent the entire afternoon luxuriating in the Romantic beauty of Castel Sant'Angelo, Hadrian's mausoleum. I'm sure the Spaniard Hadrian dreamt of having his Bithynian buried there alongside him, even though Antinous had already been dead for five years when Hadrian began the project. While I was walking near the periphery, I contemplated throwing myself to my death *à la Tosca*. I wonder what the headline in the *La Repubblica* would read, if there would be any mention of me at all, since I am a Nohbdy like your namesake, Odysseus, the man of many travels.

And as I sat there on the ledge, brooding over my mortality, I came to the realization that very few people would attend my funeral, other than the obligatory family members appearing only to honor my parents, but not from deep love for me. I am an unloved wretch, and think that you may be my sole friend in the entire world. Were I to die, you would come to my funeral, no? I refrained from hurling myself from the summit since I realized that the world would be losing too much beauty should I perish at the tender age of 21. I speak here, not of my flesh, which will inevitably decompose, but of my ageless soul, which has many more beautiful poems to compose. *Beauty, and its pursuit, is sustaining.*

After a few hours, I escaped from the Castel Sant'Angelo since it was becoming infested with British expats, and as you well know, I despise the English living in Italy. Were I dictator of Italia, I would restrict their visits to a maximum of two weeks. Incidentally, would it be in bad taste, if I wore a Napoleonic hat as the dictator of Italia? Would the Italian demos object to this? No matter, were I dictator, their opinion would not matter, so the issue is settled. Should I ever assume the mantle of Italian dictator I will parade around in a Napoleonic hat!

I am off to America tomorrow, Delray Beach, to be precise, to meet with the principals of YouthMedicale and to visit the compounding pharmacy that is nearly finished. Though I am dreading a return to Philistine, I am excited about the financial prospect as well as the illicit nature of the project; it is the 21st century version of running guns in Africa like Rimbaud! Ha! I laugh now, but I wonder how I would react should I be sentenced to prison.

-Gabriele, The Criminal,

October 5th, 2001

Dear Odysseus, wild spear-man,

The flight back to America was bumpy towards the tail end, and even more so since I was 'engaged' in the restroom with one of the Italian stewardesses. I am missing Italy already, longing for the vibrant piazza life. No one here seems to be truly alive, with people being isolated from one another, going from their respective abodes, to work, and then returning home again after eight mind-numbing hours of labor for a dreary evening of electronic isolation: idling at the television or the computer, indulging in gadget worship. What kind of existence is this? We have become masters (or is it slaves?) of technology, machines, and the steady march of progress, while the Italians have mastered the art of life! Lingering over a cup of espresso, savoring a strange kiss, walking in the open air under the moonlight. We are wealthier, they happier.

The sole aim of my life is to feel alive if only for a few fleeting moments here and there, and this is nigh impossible to achieve here in the States.   Though I have often been critical of Eliot, I seem to be trapped within his *Hollow Men*; everyone is so goddamned depressive, cynical, and lifeless. Now, before I turn into a grumpy curmudgeon railing against modern American life, I must tell you that I've eaten at least thirty ounces of beef every single day since I've been here. How happy this makes me! I even dined in one of the all-you-can-eat Brasilian steakhouses stuffing my face until I could barely stand. I wish that I could bring one of these restaurants back to Rome, along with the raven-tressed Brasilian waitresses who are as ravenous as they are delicious. Gostosas!

In fact, one of the waitresses spawned such suffering within my wild-songed soul that I was compelled to pen the poem below; for only the fevered composition of poesy or a flood of bloodletting would alleviate my insatiable longings for this lovely-locked naiad. There is divinity not only in the consummation of desire, Odysseus, but also in its savage sensations.

Sing to me, oh Pierian Muse, of my brazen desire
for a Brasilian goddess.
Desire that consumes like a bouquet of flaming fire.
Her long-flowing tresses are dressed
with wild-winged flowers flown from hidden bowers.
Her flesh is colored and contoured with bronzed amber,
brilliant and bright as bold Bahian sunlight,
and beauteous as a note of jazz swirling
in singing jasmine –
jasmine drunk on swaying moonlight.

Sing to me, oh Pierian Muse, of her entrancing mouth.
The very entrance to Eden:
A garden of sensual pleasure, an oasis of wild-sin,
A bastion of savage emotion.
Her golden lips are draped in twin

tulips twined with honey:
glimmering like glinting diamonds in the Brasilian sun
glistening like forgotten springs sprung from the sweet South
and gleaming like a soft-songed simile
stolen from Arcadian poetry.

Sing to me, oh Pierian Muse, of her lustrous, lusty eyes.
Like two cerulean sea-pearls, like two wild-growing almonds
struck by the spring-sun:
Magnificent, majestic, and radiant!
A mere glance from this exotic goddess
lances my breast – a breast that can only softly sigh.
The very sound of her voice sends pulses of Passion
coursing through my blood – like a flood of wounded
carnations,
like aurorean light streaming through the dreamy firmament,
like autumnal shade shattering a summery solstice.

Oh, how I suffer in solitude and in silence for a single kiss!

-Gabriele, of the volcanic poesia,

October 6th, 2001

Dear Odysseus Pane, Hero of the 21st century,

  I am surely adored by the Gods on high, Odysseus! This afternoon, while idling in BellaFredos on Lincoln Road, delighting in both the pleasant Floridian sunlight and the honey-skinned feminine playthings of Miami, I chanced upon Tadeusz Mickiewicz, the world-renowned aesthetic painter. I immediately introduced myself, conveying my admiration for his refined artistic sensibility. As you well know, Odysseus, I worship him as something of a God, the closest thing modern culture has to an actual ancient Greek,

Roman, or Renaissance painter. When I finished my gushing verbal encomium, Tadeusz lit up like an oasis of lapis lazuli kissed by the glittering light of noon, or a ravine of lava glistening under the ravishing moon.

He is not used to being recognized in public as if he were an American celebrity: an actor, gladiator (athlete), business tycoon, or whatever else *those people* deify. We struck up an intense conversation over espresso, becoming immediate aesthetic allies, even conceiving the outline for a collaborative painting. We are aiming to express the Grecian concepts of *To Kalon* (The Beautiful) and *Andreia* (strength/manly courage) within one painting. So, I will pose in the heroic manner modeled on Polyclitus' 'Doryphoros' (spear-bearer), but instead of holding a spear, I will be grasping a torch, emblematic of the intellectual light that the ancient Greeks discovered, and shared with civilization, for to pursue beauty, knowledge, and wisdom is to shine light into one's soul, and into the soul of the cosmos. I would like to add a Romantic element into the painting by including Keatsian butterflies, but presently we are unsure of how to incorporate them properly. But rest assured, Odysseus, it will be a masterpiece when finished. Blessed are those who create from joy, wild and holy joy, for the glory of Olympus is theirs to behold!

-Gabriele Magnus

October 7th, 2001

Dear Odysseus, wily in speech,

I was almost murdered yesterday afternoon! I was driving to a former lover of mine's home, Carmen, a beatific Cuban lingerie model who lives in Hialeah, whose parents were conveniently out of town. Generally when I drive, I listen to an audio recording of Homer, especially when I am heading to the gymnasia or to a tryst, so that the exploits of the heroes inspire me to preternatural physical feats.

Now, I am not sure if you are familiar with the environs of Miami, but Hialeah is something of the armpit of Miami. So, while stopped at a traffic light, I happened to glance over to see what seemed to be four young gang members staring directly at me. They were of course listening to barbarous music. So, in order to taunt them, I blared the glorious verse of Homer; they responded in kind (not with Homer, of course), whereupon I shouted at them *'Vaffanculo barbari!'*

One of them exited the car, so I did the same. I put my hands up ready to fight four of these punks by my lonesome, but as he approached he drew a 9 mm gun, pointing it at my chest. I can't tell you how relieved I was that the gun was aimed at my chest, so that if he immediately fired, I would die fully beautiful; for if he fired at my face, my lovely countenance would resemble rotten, mashed hamburger meat left to endure equatorial heat for weeks on end.

Though I have pretensions to being a God, I am but a man, experiencing fear like everyone else. So, for a split second, I contemplated fleeing. But I decided to remain, since nothing stains a man's reputation more than possessing back-wounds, and I was fairly certain that he would shoot me in my back should I flee. So, there we both stood, frozen as mannequins – immobile as two twigs encased in arctic ice. He falsely believed that his weapon would send me running like a cowardly sheep chancing upon a snarling wolf, and when I did not, he was at a loss as to how to proceed.

The fact that he falsely assumed me to be a Caucasian also played into the stalemate, since many white Americans seem to fear those with darker skin. He was not aware that he did not face a trembling American Caucasian, but a Greco-Roman God, the descendant of Herakles and Dienekes, until I held my ground like a stubborn mule. This punk very well may have his victory, I thought to myself, but he would earn it, never receiving 'earth and water' from me. He would learn, if nothing else, that my love of The Beautiful does not render me soft.

So, I did the one thing that he was not expecting: I began to taunt him, daring him to shoot me, telling him that he did not have the courage, mocking him, laughing at him. Whether it was from my taunts or from the fact that there were people in the street now watching this scene unfold, he slinked back into his car like a sly vulture retreating from a circling cheetah.

As soon as the car sped away, a young Cuban goddess, dressed in high heels, a short pink mini-skirt and a white top, a top which only accentuated the bronzed blush of her delectable skin, approached me saying, 'Wow! You were so brave! I thought for sure that he was going to shoot you dead. Come have a drink with me, you could certainly use one.' As you can surmise, Odysseus, I never made it to Carmen's house that night, but spent it with Olivia, of the olive skin, taking her three times, leaving empurpled wounds of passion upon her soft flesh, flesh as delicate and fragile as a dainty petal from a wounded flower.

-Gabriele, Don Jooan of Hialeah,

October 8th, 2001

Dear Odysseus, lying-tongued,

I am writing to you from Delray Beach, Florida, after a successful meeting with the company. I may be able to make $100,000 to $300,000 a year working with them. My hope is that I can work for a few years, earn enough money, and then extricate myself from the situation before the Feds take an interest. Maybe I will return to the isle of my ancestors, Lesbos, after my foray into pharmaceuticals. One of the owners of YouthMedicale accumulated the lion's share of his wealth from pornographic internet websites, claiming that he makes $200,000 a month – yes, a month, not a year!

My God, can you imagine the library that I could construct with such money? It would rival the far-famed Alexandrian library burned by the Romans. We could even launch our own boutique literary press modeled on 'Kalon' in Milan with such an exorbitant amount of gold. This way we would not have to kowtow to publishers like pathetic paupers with outstretched hands – we would have true intellectual independence and freedom – lesser minds would not control our fate!

I must confess that I feel like a foreigner, a metoikos, here in America. I do think that would be a fitting title for a poem – *A Metoikos in America* – what do you think? I am longing for my return tonight to divine Rome, my soul's home. I have now adopted Roman mannerisms to such a degree that whenever I order a simple meal here in America my hand gestures and intense gaze frighten the poor waitress. I have to tone down my movements, which are interpreted by the Americans as hyper aggressive, yet are commonplace in Roma.

But I vow to you in this very epistle, Odysseus, that I will never condescend to becoming an American, even if I do eventually settle here permanently. I will never idle on a couch, drinking beer, eating potato chips, while watching cars circle around an oval race-track for hours on end. While I was here, I had the pleasure of meeting a scholar of Italian culture, Dr. Praz. We chatted over an espresso, while incessantly discussing all things relating to glorious Italia. The meeting made me very happy, knowing that even in Philistine there are some who still appreciate The Beautiful. I hope to continue my correspondence with him, and even enroll in one of his courses upon my return to university.

My erotic overtures were rebuffed today by an American woman who protested that she first must go on three dates with a man before she even contemplates physical entanglement. Can you imagine this rubbish? A proper Roman contessa would have tasted me several times by the time this priggish woman finished her prolix rationale for her arbitrary three date rule. Though I admit that I suffer from the excesses of passion, and am no thing to be admired or emulated, these Americans do not possess one iota of passion and are as frigid as an Englishman exiled in Siberia. I cannot wait to take my passeggiata tomorrow evening, whereupon I will transform from an American 'bar-bar' back into a denizen of Rome!

-Gabriele, Fool of Passion,

October 14th, 2001

Dear Odysseus, King of the Gauls,

I apologize for the delay in writing, but travel weeks are always trying. I am writing to you from Piazza di Spagna, which is a beautiful piazza (though aren't they all here in Italy?), especially on Sundays when the entire piazza is filled with many-colored flowers, flowers whose scents are as succulent as a heaven-sent maiden dancing in an Arcadian garden. What a beautiful life I have! I can idle in this piazza doing nothing of consequence – people-watching, reading, and sipping espresso before taking a 'Keats-Shelley break' since the museum is located here.

The Italians call my state of blissful indolence *'il dolce far niente,'* translated as 'the sweetness of doing nothing.' The supreme goal of my life is to somehow become a master of this pursuit. Let others become accomplished and adulated, I just wish to partake in the pleasure of doing nothing, being nothing – completely free – forgotten by society to where former friends and acquaintances wonder aloud to each other, 'Whatever became of Gabriele? Is he still alive?'

To live this life of a haughty Italian flâneur, a dissipated Roman Prince, is so utterly desirable – given solely to the Lesbian lyre, to the whims of my soul, and to the fire of passion, very soon consumed by its amber-hued embers, with members of my family left only to sigh and lament: 'If only he had dedicated himself to something noble, he would have then become an admirable man, but as it stands, he is nothing more than an admonition for others, an object of perverse wonder, an exemplar of wasted potential.'

Just a short time ago, I spent twenty minutes kissing an impassioned Roman girl. Her lush lips, flush with honey, and shaped like twin crescent moons, are the quintessence of beauty. When struck by the light of the sun, they sparkle as if sprinkled with thousands of finely crushed diamonds – diamonds thin as grains of sand, yet brilliant as solar streams brimming with jasmine. I dressed her dark tresses with flowers before kissing her, so that I experienced the pleasure proffered from her dewy kisses, coupled with the dreamy aroma of the freshly-bloomed flowers. At times, I even pressed a few carefully chosen rose petals between our entangled lips. *Oh, the Pleasure! The Pleasure!* I engaged in this partly for the sensual pleasure to be derived from kissing a young girl's snow-soft lips, and partly to horrify the Anglo-American tourists, who are aghast at public displays of affection, so often indulged in by the Italians.

-Gabriele, lover of flowers and young girls, (but not too young, of course)

October 15th, 2001

Dear Odysseus, quick-tongued,

Zarathustra is suffering from a syphilis headache! Thus spake Gabriele!

-Zarathustra

October 16th, 2001

Dear Odysseus, double-tongued,

I have been receiving nearly two letters of adoration a day from my female admirers. Here is one that will make you giggle to yourself.

> *Gabriele,*
>
> *I want to worship on my knees. . . you are the most beautiful man that I've ever seen, and just the mere mention of your name makes me shiver. Gabriele! Gabriele! Gabriele! When my friend showed me the picture of you and the Greek statue, I nearly fainted. I can't believe how close the resemblance is. Wars have been waged over chests like yours!*
>
> *If you would allow me, I would be honored to worship you. I have all sorts of dark fantasies in my mind that I've been too shy to experience with any of my previous Lovers, but I feel that you may be the*

perfect man to let go with. I have enclosed a collar and leash with this letter that I wish you to place on me, should we ever meet.

Your obedient servant,
Chiara

Oh, how I tire of erotic dalliances, Odysseus. Is sensual pleasure the sole aim of our existence? Is there nothing more to life than perfumed tresses, milky thighs, and silk-soft kisses? You are probably laughing, worried that I may become some sort of cloistered monk in the near future, but even though I have these moral thoughts occasionally, the pull of the flesh is still too strong for me to renounce 'idoni.'

With each passing day, my desire to travel to Greece increases. Some of my extended family owns a hotel in Mytilene, Lesbos, so perhaps I can finagle a free room, or in the least, a discounted rate. Lesbos, of the lovely dances, would be a prime location to build an army against the Turks, since on a clear day one can see Turkey off in the distance. How Romantic it would be to live on the same isle as my poetic ancestors, Sappho and Alcaeus!

I can think of few things more pleasurable than to lie under the Grecian sun in some hidden hillock completely 'gymnos,' bathed in freshly-pressed olive oil, garlanded in wild-growing vines, reading Homer aloud to a few fair-colored flowers; flowers whose petals serve as hammocks for the soft-winged butterflies of Lesbos. And every so often, I would cease reading, so as to gaze upon the sun-flushed horizon, out towards far-renowned Troy, dreaming of fighting alongside the Homeric heroes of old.

-Gabriele, of the Homeric Soul,

October 18th, 2001

Odysseus, swift-tongued,

I am always very careful that I do not impregnate any of my harem-women, for that would be the death of me. I can barely support myself, and cannot imagine the horrific poverty that would befall me should such a disaster arise. Furthermore, I think that the Gods would punish my excessive philandering by cursing me with a promiscuous daughter, a modern Valeria Messalina. The Gods, like the moderns, love irony, no?

However, were I to have a daughter, I would place her in a convent to shield her from men like myself. Perhaps with the proper rearing, she would then become the next Mother Teresa. I'd only consent to having children, if I could provide a modest trust fund for them, so that they could thoroughly escape the drudgery of a work-a-day existence, having the financial wherewithal to pursue their passions, which I hope would be of the intellectual persuasion.

This stance stands diametrically opposed to the American ethos that employment for its own sake somehow enriches the soul. Even many in the American moneyed elite force their children to embark upon a dutiful career instead of allowing them to live fabulously on their trust fund. These are people who boast at toney cocktail parties, 'I have fifteen million dollars sitting in my bank account, but my son is scraping by in a one bedroom, working 60 hours a week, and he won't see a penny until I'm dead.'

I simply do not understand such madness! Do these people not know that we all have but one life to live? Why would parents compel their children to waste even one single second in toil to a stranger instead of giving them the ability to live powerfully and fully, if they have the means? I am in agreement with Aristotle when he correctly noted that *'All paid jobs absorb and degrade the mind.'* Well, I would revise it slightly adding 'most' instead of the sweeping 'all.' If one is able somehow to turn one's passion into employment, there would be no real conflict. Do you think my above statement is merely self-serving, silly rationale for falling into my current state of luxurious lassitude?

Anyhow, let me now return to the proposition of parenthood. My only real wish would be that my children would not have an artistic temperament, condemned to suffer obscurity and poverty; instead, let them become an accountant, a mathematician, a computer programmer, or something of the sort, if circumstance necessitated some kind of employment.

-Gabriele, The Capitalist,

October 19th, 2001

Dear Odysseus, slayer of Laestrygones,

The other evening while seated in a café, I overheard two women discussing my beautiful body, and I couldn't help but thinking: *'Ah, if only they could see my soul, how they would marvel then!'* It is something of a tragedy that one spends so much time in refinement of the body, only for it to eventually decay and die. Yet, what is one to do, in the meanwhile – simply wait for death? I wish to cram one thousand lives into this one, since I have yet to be convinced of the prospect of reincarnation. I know that I often bombard you with unanswerable questions, but I've always held the belief that a wise man has more questions than answers, no?

Now, I am going to reveal to you my successful method of seducing beautiful women in cafes. When a lovely young thing makes her entrance into the café, most of the men gape like a ménagerie of drooling baboons, or a pound of panting hound dogs, but you must resist this natural urge. You must not only refrain from staring at her, but your demeanor must also be tinged with a hint of detached hauteur, as if it is beneath your dignity to meet her gaze. She will undoubtedly notice this, finding you mysterious, wondering to herself: 'Why hasn't he stared at me like the rest of the men? Is he gay? Does he not find me beautiful? Is he so devoted to another woman that he will not even gaze upon another beauty? And if this is so, how admirable! I wish that I could find such a loyal man who only has eyes for me!'

Mulling over these questions in her mind, she will drive herself mad, but you still must wait a bit, allowing one of the other men to make a failed foray first. Once she has rebuffed the impatient suitor, then and only then, can you catch her eyes a few times before uttering some inane offhand comment like *'The coffee here is shit, not like the coffee in Bangladesh,'* further confusing the poor maiden, since she has probably never been to Bangladesh, nor tasted Bangladeshi coffee. You have officially become mysterious to her. Now, more questions will dog her: 'Why was he in a place as exotic as Bangladesh? He must be wealthy. Maybe he is an international businessman? A wealthy jet-setter? A spy?'

Once you have made your statement she will certainly begin a conversation, perhaps querying you about Bangladeshi coffee, or something else, but no matter, as at that point the conquest is academic. Remember, women crave not only beauty, but mystery – give them both simultaneously, and you can have as many as your heart, or any other appendage of your body, desires.

-Gabriele, son of Casanova,

October 20th, 2001

Dear Odysseus, of the sweet tongue,

These little American critics have taken to labeling me some sort of anti-hero, which I fervently object to, for I am an idolater of heroes. Whenever I hear the term anti-hero, I think of Holden Caulfield, Leopold Bloom, or Thersites whereas I am something of Achilles, Herakles, or Childe Harold. ***History is not a nightmare from which I am trying to awaken, but rather, a glorious tale which I wish to be cast in.*** If anything, the proper characterization of me would be the 'hero-villain,' but most certainly not the anti-hero.

Yet, what can one expect from these American critics who have no real sense of or interest in *To Kalon*. In fact, these snarky cynics seem to revel in setting fire to the 'flowers of Arcady,' yet you and I, Odysseus, will spend our entire lives replanting those flowers, eh? These are people who eschew rhyme and any sort of form in poesia – *bar bar bar bar bar bar bar* – my god! One may as well argue for disallowing the presence of the sun in the divine rise of the rosy-fingered dawn, or position oneself against the use of color in painting. Let me say it again – *bar bar bar bar bar bar!*

I spent the last few hours reading through the excerpts of your novel in progress, and I must congratulate you for the work thus far – it is very beautiful, and I would venture to say that it transcends the mere label of prose since it contains the very roses of poesy. What will you title it? I think '*Parisian Reveries*' would be apropos, no? Over the past week, I've been contemplating my future, if I manage to survive into full adulthood, making it into retirement, and assuming my inheritance. Besides giving myself to introspective, intellectual pursuits, penning works in the manner of Marcus Aurelius' *Meditations*, I would have two other real interests, I think. The first would be collecting art, of the aesthetic variety, of course, while the second would be funding a gladiatorial school – Ludus Paterkallos – where I would possess a stable of young boxers, fit as lions, competing for gold, glory, and women.

-Gabriele, The Hero-Villain,

October 21st, 2001

Dear Odysseus, raider of cities,

Last evening, I wandered alone through the streets of Rome like a drunken gypsy in search of nothing, but hungering for everything. I simply roamed for the melancholic pleasure of embarking upon a richly woven Roman odyssey. I spent many hours gazing upon the ardent moon – Yes, *the moon! The moon!* That sliver of silver that hangs like a curved icicle dangling from a hidden elm. And this morning as dawn with her fingertips of shivering rose arose in the eastern sky, I found myself in the Janiculum Hill beneath the equestrian statue of great-souled Garibaldi, the fiery revolutionary who helped to free Italy from foreign masters. What a man! What a hero! His famous saying *'Qui si fa l'Italia o si muore'* – *'Here we make Italy, or we die!'* – is divine.

It seems to me, Odysseus, heroes like Garibaldi do not exist any longer, as they have been emasculated by modernity. What do you think? Are there any heroes left? And are we fools for dreaming of heroism in the 21st century when our peers are mired in irony, cynicism, and minimalism? Here I go again, my Parisian friend, with my series of tendentious questions. After hero-worshipping Garibaldi, I simply reveled in the gorgeous view afforded by the Janiculum Hill. The bright light brimmed over the horizon like a golden cauldron spilling Samian wine. What a glorious sight!

Though I am a writer, I cannot fully express in any language the raptures and ecstasies that the view of Rome inspires within my soul, as if the flaring fires of the stars, the flaming lava of Vesuvius, and the furious blood of the sun all simultaneously collide upon my breast forming a grand conflagration! A war of beauty and passion! Oh, how I long to remain in Rome forever! The prospect of having to return to Philistine overwhelms me with such sorrow that I collapse into the dark earth as a wounded tree when gently touched by a mere whisper of purring wind.

But just as despair with its sickly talons began to pierce my breast, I heard the faint strain of the Cretan lyra. Sitting beneath the Manfredi Lighthouse was a stout, swarthy Cretan playing his lyra, singing to the freshly risen sun with its spangled petals full of angled light. I am embarrassed to confess that I could not understand a single word since I have lost the Grecian tongue, yet I must assure you however that my soul remains as Hellenic as Leonidas' himself. The song was rich in beauty and passion (aren't all of the Greek songs?), moving my soul from the depths of despair to the summit of ecstasy! I listened to him for countless hours as the sun made its daily ascent into the timeless Roman firmament, blessing us, and the demos alike, with its holy light.

-Gabriele, son of Garibaldi,

October 24th, 2001

Dear Odysseus, godlike man,

I've attached a photograph taken yesterday at the gymnasia with this missive to illustrate just how far my body has come with my illicit 'supplements.' I now weigh 220 lbs from my original 200 lbs. The gymnasia owner is actually arranging a photo shoot with one of the leading Italian fitness magazines. He also mentioned that a producer friend of his is doing a show for the American TV program *'Real Life'* on bodybuilding and steroids; he wanted to know if I had any interest in doing such a thing. As you well know, it is beneath my literary genius to do something so common, something targeted solely for the rabble, but if nothing else it would probably allow me to seduce *even* more soft-eyed young maidens. Playing the role of the villain also attracts me, since I will be the steroid-using (well, in society's eyes 'steroid-abusing') rogue who deliberately and unapologetically flaunts conventional mores.

This afternoon I brooded about the Trevi Fountain doing my best Marcello impression. Gazing upon Nicola Salvi's masterpiece, further confirmed my love for the baroque, in all of its various forms. I am America's only avowed baroque poet with the vast majority of my contemporaries (they are most certainly not my peers!) mired in minimalism. Let them remain in Iowa gushing over W.C. Williams, while I, me, Gabriele Paterkallos, stand beneath the marble-wreathed Trevi Fountain composing phrases such as 'the sea-shimmering sea-spray reflects the raging rays of Helios/on the comely coast of lovely Lesbos.' More is more, Odysseus. Here I go again on yet another literary rant, which I'm sure bores you to death, much preferring my licentious exploits.

Well, here is another tawdry anecdote for you then, Mr. Pane. Do you remember the letter from Chiara with the enclosed collar and leash? Well, for the last two days, I kept her as my private slave, completely nude, wearing only her collar and leash on all occasions – she fixed my food, bathed me, and as you can imagine, did anything, and let me stress that just a bit more – *anything* – that my depraved imagination fancied. I will not relay the specifics in this letter, as they are much too graphic for prose, but rest assured that Alcibiades himself blushed. She now wishes to continue this wanton game, remaining collared and bound in chains, becoming my permanent concubine. Ha! My god, soon I will be forced to renounce my Hellenic blood dressing myself as The Sultan of Rome! *Ah, the Pleasure! The Pleasure!*

-Gabriele, The Sultan,

October 27th, 2001

Dearest Odysseus, literary Titan,

I now write to you from the environs of Magna Grecia, Poseidonia, or as the moderns would say, Paestum, where some of the best preserved Grecian temples remain. Southern Italy and Sicily contain the glimmering gems still shining from the immortal diadem of Hellenic architecture. The barbarous Turks ravaged Greece proper hoping to eradicate any permanent remains of the glorious Hellenic dream; they failed, of course, since they could only burn the monuments of Hellenism, but not the indomitable Grecian soul. Oh, how I long to wage war against the Turks! With my herculean body, I could slay twenty armed, emaciated Asiatics with my bare hands.

But enough of my foolish braggadocio, let us return to my idyllic surroundings. A serene tranquility overtakes my soul as I stand before the ancient temples, for the monuments still retain a curative power unblemished by the passage of time. I have an insistent urge to sing rhythmic hymns to Athena and Poseidon, hoping that my earnest entreaties awaken them from their slumber. Trust me, Pan yet lives, he just needs a bit of prodding! Also, I must confess that although I generally prefer the baroque, I find the Doric simplicity of these temples entrancing. I simply cannot pull my gaze from their monumental grandeur.

I long to strip off my clothes, oil my body, and lift gargantuan rocks so as to both honor and compete with the Gods themselves until I collapse from exhaustion. And standing before the Temple of Hera, I had the wild dream of teaching myself ancient Greek, composing all of my poesia in the language of Homer and Sappho. Oh, to speak the language of heroes and Gods! Even if this task took me fifty years to achieve, I do think that it would be an honorable endeavor. Yet, just as I was drifting off into phantasmal realms of gold lined with timeless Homeric similes, a troupe of smiling school-girls arrived, so you can imagine how the scene ended.

-Gabriele, citizen of Poseidonia,

October 28th, 2001

Il Mio Caro Amico, Odysseus,

In the Hotel Lobby here in Paestum just before my departure, I was cornered into a conversation with a few American expats, who on the whole are generally more tolerable than the British variety. One of them remarked, *'Ah Gabriele, you are a Romantic, an old soul.'* Yet I could not disagree more with this assessment. My soul may be ancient, but it is not old in the least.

In fact, it is as young as a freshly-bloomed rose-petal in Arcadia enduring its first blaze of liquid light – as young as a baby butterfly embarking on its virginal flight – as young as newly born dew before it is overcome by the rose-drawn-dawn in its furious might. Though I will undoubtedly age, my body wrinkling and sagging, my hair thinning and even disappearing, my soul will always be beautiful and youthful.

-Gabriele, of the ancient Soul,

October 29th, 2001

Dear Odysseus, lover of the lyre,

I am staying at the Villa Lamaro in Sorrento on the Amalfi Coast. Sorrento, Positano, and Amalfi are the three most prominent towns on this scenic stretch of shoreline. Driving on the sinuous roads that hug the mountains like a serpentine river snaking through a sheer rock-face, while gazing out at the Neapolitan Bay is simply stunning; beyond stunning, to be exact. The Amalfi Coast is so beautiful that one needs to invent new adjectives in order to properly describe it – adjectives related to 'splendiferous' – adjectives like 'phosphorgasmic.'

The entire villa is a diadem fallen from heaven, but the crown-jewel is the view from the balcony. It towers over the Neapolitan Bay like a castle overlooking its vast domain. I sit here for hours on end listening to music and reading. The villas here are nestled high within the mountains, so one is closer to the Gods than to men it seems – closer to one's dreams than to one's reality; in fact, wisps of clouds literally float by, and I, of course, cannot resist the urge to touch them, to kiss them even. I have often been accused by the modern literati, one could simply say modern castrati, of having my 'head in the clouds,' mumbled as some sort of pejorative, but now I finally have my revenge, Odysseus. For while they lie in the gutter hissing like a sneering coterie of snakes, I am literally dancing in the clouds as if I were Dionysus himself, or in the very least, one of his devoted satyrs! Ha! Miserable peasants!

One sometimes expects a choir of winged angels to be carried in on the following gust of wind. The dual view of the mountains and the sea elevates the Amalfi Coast from 'the picturesque' to that of 'the divine.' Have you ever lived among the clouds in some castle-like villa, Odysseus? If not, it is certainly something that you must experience someday. The pace of life here is very slow, which is a welcome respite from a city, but I do think that if I lived here permanently, I would miss the vibrant energy and the cultural opportunities of Rome.

-Gabriele, man of the clouds,

October 30th, 2001

Dear Odysseus, Homeric warrior,

I am writing to you from the most beautiful place on the planet – the belvedere, or the Terrace of Infinity in Villa Cimbrone. Every so often I pinch myself as a reminder that I am still mortal and have not somehow ascended into heaven. On my left is a columned archway, while a series of heroic busts rest in front of me, with the horizon just beyond, a horizon where the sea and the sky seem to be engaged in an impassioned dance, in an everlasting kiss, where they have come to be one single being, completely inseparable from the other.

Nothing has so convinced me of the existence of the Gods more than this moment here in Villa Cimbrone. Talk to me no more of words, of points, and counterpoints, of Reason – for this view alone has converted me into a faithful believer.

-Gabriele, The Believer,

November 2nd, 2001

Dear Odysseus, Bane of Troy,

Upon my triumphant return to Rome, I was greeted with another letter from Richard Joya, the 31-year-old American poet residing in Boca Raton, Florida. He informed me that he is launching his own publishing company and offered to publish any of my future books should I have an interest. I salute this man for his pioneering endeavor, for many of the American smaller poetry presses are run by 'barbaroi' with such logos as a skull and crossbones, a wilted flower, or a Duchampian latrine.

Can you imagine how Walter Pater must be rolling in his grave? Do you want to know what Mr. Joya's logo consists of? A butterfly resting on a rose petal. Ah, how audacious! How revolutionary in 2001 to do such a thing! I love this man, Joya, and if anything goes awry with my publisher here in Rome, I will support him.

I know that you are beholden to 'GoldenRoom' in Paris, but if you ever have a falling out with them, keep Joya in mind. The world needs more men with his sensibility. Try as I might, Odysseus, I cannot seem to pull my eyes away from his logo: a dreamy butterfly resting on a rose petal. Oh, if only I could be reincarnated as an Italian butterfly – flying into the sun-fluttering gardens of Positano – beauty incarnate!

But now let us leave beatific Positano for malefic New York. Have you also noticed that New York intellectuals, and the culture at large, seem to be enthralled with the middling writing of the smug, William Hitcher, the noted anti-theist? The all-knowing Hitcher sneers at those who do not also possess his animus for organized religion; he and his gaggle of militant atheists seem to be intent on playing the role of iconoclasts (in the truest definition of the word). As you know, Odysseus, I am not a Galilean by any stretch of the imagination, but do not muddy my name by associating me with these pompous nihilists. In fact, just to get their goat, I should compose an essay titled *The Necessity of Belief.*

Though at times I have had my doubts, I do believe in the presence of the Gods. For me, it is not something that I can prove through the limits of Reason, but rather, it is a feeling of the soul. When I gaze upon a lushly colored flower flushed with streaked-carmine, the blushing sun in its crepuscular glare, or a child's shy smile, I can feel the presence of divinity. Let others demand to see a burning bush, a flowering one has convinced me. But simply because I believe in the Gods' existence, does not mean that I adhere to the common belief that they have any real interest in our endeavors. In fact, it might be the height of all human vanity to fancy that the Gods on high are concerned with the petty affairs of men, though I do hope that I am wrong about this, of course. Irrespective of the veracity of my thought, one must surely savor every ephemeral sensation of life, for our time on earth may well be the full totality of our experience.

By the bye, I almost forgot to mention that I have accepted an amateur boxing match this coming Saturday. It is a very small venue with approximately 50 people in attendance, mostly lower-class eastern Europeans. In fact, a local Romanian pimp is the organizer of the event – he has agreed to pay me $100 for the fight plus $100 more should I be victorious. I plan to step into the ring garlanded in wild-growing wildflowers with Cretan lyra music playing in the background; perhaps, I can have some of his jezebels dance behind me as I make my entrance, playing the obedient maenads to my Dionysus. Ah, how I wish you were here to see this spectacular spectacle! Before I leave you, Odysseus, let me share with you a fragment of a letter from one of my ever-growing legion of female devotees.

Her body is tense and primed for battle, the greater the pleasure in being cut down and weakened with softest sweetness, that just a word, from a man who could break her with his eyes, snap her body with his hands, is all that is required...to make her... submissive.

His name sends a spear of shivers straight through her core, that she loves the piercing and drives it deeper, repeating over and over again, Gabriele, Gabriele, Gabriele Paterkallos. . . first a whimper, then a moan, then a verbal spasm harsher than the sight of the wounding, which does not satisfy, but only intensifies the agony. . . the incessant throbbing to his name, Gabriele. . . Paterkallos. . . .

-Gabriele, The Idol,

November 4th, 2001

Dear Odysseus, Hero of Paris,

    The fight last night was a total disaster. It was a scheduled five rounder, and I dominated the emaciated gypsy that they put before me throughout, dropping him to the canvas three times in the third round alone, yet the judges awarded him the victory. Surely, the Romanian pimp, Yann, fixed the fight, so that he and his cronies could profit from the gambling action. A mini-riot ensued with a gang of men attacking Yann's coterie, with two of them even being stabbed.

I had to fight my way out of the venue, since some in the audience assumed that I had been complicit in the fraud. I knocked out three gypsies cold before making my way from the auditorium. On top of the indignity suffered from having my victory taken from me coupled with the difficulty in 'exiting the stage,' I never received my hundred dollars. I swear to you Odysseus that if I see that base-born gypsy, Yann, on the Via Salaria plying his 'trade,' I am going to beat him senseless in broad daylight, embarrassing him in front of his prostitutes.

But let us move on from these common tales to ones of great import – our war against the Turks. I've decided that after our victory in Cyprus, I will build a temple to Ares to commemorate our glorious triumph over The Barbarians. I will have my hand-selected architects model it on the ones found in Paestum. I even think that I will adopt the Roman triumphal procession, allowing my men to walk through the liberated streets of Nicosia, while the masses throw dreamy flowers and summery kisses upon them. Ah, what a beautiful thought!

After The Triumph, I will offer the services of my surviving Greeks and philhellenes to the Americans to assist them in the hunting of Xerxes, errrr, Bin Laden. For it is incumbent upon every Greek, or in the least, one with a Grecian soul, to defend the ideal of freedom from the continual onslaught of tyranny, manifested in this particular instance as an intolerant theocracy. Yes, let the fascistic Islamists, hell-bent on establishing an expanding caliphate, know that Gabriele and his army of freedom-loving Greeks are coming to 'martyr' the lot of them.

A few evenings ago, I came to the conclusion that the young lions of Crete should fill the lion's share of our army. The Cretans, valiant and defiant, are the symbolic heirs to the ancient Spartans with their fierce opposition to the Nazi invasion attesting to this. While the rest of Europe kowtowed to the marauding sons of the Huns, the Cretans resisted bravely against overwhelming odds, with even women and children joining in the struggle. To me, the Cretans seem more feral than the other Greeks, excepting perhaps the Maniots (the blood-descendants of the Spartans), with their isolation undoubtedly enabling them to thwart the trappings of modernity that has so weakened their countrymen; their martial spirit will be a definite advantage, for they will fight like a battalion of wild-charging beasts when unleashed upon The Barbarians in battle.

And let us now transition from the pursuit of glory to the pursuit of pleasure. Last night, after extricating myself from the melee, I seduced a young Brasilian woman named Liliana who is here in Rome to study ancient Roman History. My God, she is as beautiful as Aphrodite herself – a proper goddess – and as passionate as an Italian. I have a propensity for Brasilian women, for just like Italians they marry beauty, elegance, and sensuality, an irresistible combination for me. Sometimes I contemplate placing myself in self-exile not in Rome, but in Brasil, where the women are a wonder, thrusting myself between the willing legs of as many women as will have me until I invariably perish from the ravages of syphilis.

Would you ever consider leaving Paris for Brasil? Liliana is from Cascavel Parana, but I've heard that Salvador, Bahia, has the fairest ménagerie of fair-tressed, soft-breasted, feminine gems, so I think that we should settle there should we move to Brasil. Also, no culture consumes more beef than the Brasilians, so we will be as strong as Homeric Greeks from the copious amounts of protein consumed. What more could any man desire?

-Gabriele, The one who fights with untamed Beasts,

November 5th, 2001

Dear Odysseus, great tactician,

I spent the entire day in the Vatican Museum with my publisher, Gianluca. It was my third visit to the museum during my extended stay here. I do feel that if I lived in Rome, I would make the excursion at least once a month as an aesthetic pilgrimage of sorts, for I never tire of standing before the immortal works of Michelangelo, Raphael, and various other Masters.

My personal favorite is the sculpture *'Hercules of the Forum Boarium,'* which I much prefer to the more renowned *'Farnese Hercules.'* The *'Hercules of the Forum Boarium'* is rendered in gilded bronze, so one can only imagine how it must have gleamed under the ancient sun before it was weathered by the bane of time and neglect. Though one could argue that the now aged, muted bronze adds a nostalgic element to the sculpture – there is something beautiful in the breakdown, no? Herakles holds a club in his right hand, an apple in his left, while the Nemean lion-skin drapes his left forearm. As I stand before him, I have the urge to honor his godlike form, yet also to rival his strength and beauty, even becoming his superior. It is the same sentiment that Alexander must have felt standing before ancient depictions of death-dealing, Achilles, on the wall-frescoes of Pella.

I must train harder in the gymnasia, Odysseus, so that I can stand as an equal before Herakles himself, challenging him to single combat in either boxing, wrestling, or pankration (literally, all-powers), or as the moderns like to say, mixed-martial-arts. Or maybe instead of opposing him, we will join together to liberate the Cypriots from barbarian incursion. Yes, that is much more heroic – instead of becoming adversaries, we will become allies, creating our own 'mythos' through our glorious deeds.

After the Vatican Museum jaunt, I had a tryst with one of my Italian women here named Francesca, who speaks absolutely no English, an attribute which I much prefer, since I generally do not get on with an intellectual woman. Sometimes I close my eyes, and listen to her speak endlessly, so as to delight in the mellifluous symphonies flowing from her tongue. I instruct her to speak about anything that strikes her fancy, just so that I can revel in the aural beauty springing from her singing lips. And I aver that there are few things in this world more beautiful than the sound of the Italian language, especially when sung by a honeyed-tongued young woman.

You may disagree with me here, declaring French a more beautiful language. I too adore the savory sound of the French language, but find it at times to be too frigid, too formal, too intellectual, lacking the fire, the lava, and the earthy gesticulations inherent in Italian. But I do digress, so let us return to bronze-armed, olive-skinned Francesca. My favorite moments with her are just before she climaxes; when her entire body trembles like wind-kissed water; when her eyelashes flutter like the wild wings of a frightened starling; and when she begins to scream in frenzied Italian, always finishing with... *'Dammi il latte! Dammi il latte!'* until she finally climbs the sublime summit of ecstasy. *Oh, the Pleasure! The Pleasure!* How can I return to America and to American women after this?

-Gabriele, the megalomaniacal dreamer,

November 8th, 2001

Dear Odysseus, man of twists and turns,

Though at times, I prefer being nigh 'gymnos' in my athletic shorts and a stringer tank top, I also derive pleasure from accoutering myself in the manner of fin-de-siecle dandies – wearing my black pinstripe suit topped with my broad-brimmed fedora. I strut about the Roman streets in the manner of Caravaggio daring anyone to knock the chip from my heroic shoulders.

I had my revenge yesterday on Yann, the Romanian gypsy. I found him just as I expected on Via Salaria surrounded by his demimonde. I hit him with a five punch combination, putting him flat on his back, whereupon I reached into his pocket taking the $200 that the shifty gypsy owed me. I spit on him, before telling him that we're now even. The comical part about the scenario was that while most of his women scattered like a gaggle of gazelles spying an angry lion, one of his women defended him, jumping on my back, scratching my neck and the like. I just shrugged her off, for as you know I would never hit a woman.

But were I Yann, I would marry this feisty gazelle, this modern Penthesilea, since she has proven that she will defend him to the death. Her nails have left terrible scratch marks upon my neck, which will probably take a good two weeks to fully heal; hopefully they will not leave a permanent scar, and if they do, I cannot reveal that they were given to me by an enraged woman. Can you imagine the rank embarrassment? I will tell the tall tale that they were given to me in Africa by a ferocious lioness during my travels with Herakles!

And while we are on the topic of lions, I've always had a fantasy of fighting as a gladiator in the Colosseum against a wild lion, yet I have no desire to harm such a lovely animal. I would simply subdue him to the point where he became docile enough to mount; thereby riding him through the gates of the Colosseum into the streets of Rome, greeting the Roman citizens with the rousing roar of my new leonine friend. And then let the plebeians say, *'there is prideful Gabriele, the strong-limbed gladiator, the one who rides upon the manes of lions!'*

-Gabriele, the narcissistic solipsist,

November 9th, 2001

Dear Odysseus, man of many-tongues,

I am sitting on the steps leading up to the Pons Fabricius, the oldest bridge in Rome; it was built in 62 BC, the year following Cicero's consulship, by Lucius Fabricius, and has been in use ever since. How poetic it is that I am in the very place where the distinguished men of Rome once walked! Perhaps Ovid or Virgil, lost in lunar raptures, composed one of their storied stanzas on these steps. Being immersed in antiquity fires my already burning ambition, as when a group of small boys toss a handful of twigs upon a flickering flame. I resolve, right here and now, to be great or nothing at all!

I am planning on spending the rest of the evening in euphoric worship of the moon. *La luna! La luna!* The turquoise moon, drunk with beauteous light tonight, is slightly touched with a hint of ruddy azure, as if brushed with whiffs of astral color. Oh, if only I were a painter, Odysseus! I would spend my entire artistic existence interpreting the multifarious colors of that spherical wonder. But before I give myself fully to the full moon like an obedient lover to soft kisses and caresses, I will share with you my thought on Rome. I view Rome as the most sensual city on the planet. Do not confuse my label 'sensual' with 'sexual' though it is most certainly that too. No other city gives such pleasure to all of the combined senses: sight, smell, hear, taste, and touch.

What could enchant the eyes more than standing beneath Michelangelo's *Sistine Chapel*, or Raphael's *School of Athens*? What aroma is sweeter than inhaling the sweet-smelling flowers arrayed in Piazza di Spagna, or stumbling into a nondescript trattoria in the Trastevere rich with the sumptuous scent of freshly-picked herbs simmering in olive oil? What is more delectable than to hear the immortal arias of Puccini and Rossini sung by fiery-eyed gypsies as one walks through the historic streets? What gratifies the palette more than biting into a piping hot piece of pizza or into a dripping ball of home-made mozzarella? And what elicits more rapture than running one's fingers across the milky white thighs of a silken-tressed maiden? How poetic it is that Roma is the Latin word for love – amor – spelled backwards. Oh Roma! Oh Amor! Oh Love!

But after having said all of this, I must reveal that the weather has changed for the worse – my Greco-Italian blood is craving the sun-ravished sands of pagan Miami where the most beautiful Brasilian, Italian, and Parisian women frolic in the frothy ocean like the nymphs and naiads from antiquity. How I despise frigid northern climes, longing for the blinding, blazing light of Helios to once again lash my skin with his heavenly spears, spears of splendid light blessed by Zeus himself. Oh, how I yearn for the sun! Let us one day build a gilded chariot to conquer the skies like my ancestor Icarus, hurling ourselves towards the immense, immolating star – like a hurtling comet aimed at the ultimate target – basking in the sun's feverish glory until the envious Olympians punish us for our overweening hubris!

I've been lost in lyra music for the last seven hours. At times, when I am very lonely and melancholy, I will listen to the lyra, gamboling about the room, banging spoons together, pounding my chest, and even taunting the Gods themselves. Were it not for the divine lyra, I would have penned seventeen books of poetry by now, but I have 'wasted' days (perhaps months) of my life simply languishing in the majestic grandeur of the lyra, unable to pull myself away! Come dance with me under the Roman moon, Odysseus! *Opa! Opa!*

-Gabriele, the Roman Sensualist,

November 10th, 2001

Dear Odysseus, wise in counsel,

I have drawn the blinds and have not ventured outside at all today. Sometimes I am overcome by the prospect of enduring too much beauty. Though it gives me such intense pleasure, it also causes immense suffering in my soul. Does your heightened sensitivity to *To Kalon* ever affect you in this way? Am I mad?

I just feel that the pain would be too pronounced today should I see a streak of swirling sunlight streaming across the soft cheek of youthful maiden, a bouquet of buoyant flowers swaying in the wild wind, or hear the tender murmuring of a soft-winged nightingale. The rabble cannot understand such things, for they have no sense of beauty, no sense of how one suffers in its presence.

-Gabriele, the Beautiful Sufferer,

November 12th, 2001

Dear Odysseus, lover of the Sirens,

Every morning I begin my day with twenty raw oysters, four quail eggs, and an entire juiced beet. This carnal concoction makes me as virile as a lusty bull denied the pleasure of mating with his harem of heifers for days on end. One hour after consuming this Cyprian dish, I prepare a whey protein shake judiciously blended with four raw chicken eggs. One does not simply become a God, Odysseus, one must Will himself to the pinnacle of Olympus!

I received a unique marriage proposal last evening, which I am presently pondering. After concluding one of my many ménages a trois with two lingerie models, one of them proposed the idea of marriage, or at least mutual cohabitation; they are a couple, so I would be a Caesar with two empresses. I would have the right to play with whomever I fancied, or both at any given moment. Maria is part Colombian and part Cuban, while Amalia is fully Swedish – both are delicious as chocolate and sweet as honey.

I rather enjoy the fact that one is dark-skinned, while the other is fair-skinned, hence affording me some variety in matters of the flesh. It is very tempting, to say the least, but I think that I must decline this offer, since I cannot consent to the slavery of fidelity, even this debauched form of fidelity. I cannot be beholden to anyone, or anything, and must be as free as a lion stalking the golden African savanna hunting for new prey. Do you think me a wanton fool or a wise man for spurning these stunning goddesses?

My satire is a sprawling mess presently, with me satirizing Eliot and Bukowski concurrently, but in time it will certainly coalesce into a masterpiece. Though the finished piece will not have a large commercial appeal, I do think that it will be a work of everlasting genius! Please do continue sharing vignettes from your novel. Your prose is so poetic, so musical, both anomalies in modern Letters, with the literary culture demanding an 'economy of prose.' *Bar bar bar bar bar bar!* Once you publish it with 'GoldenRoom,' I will send a certified letter to the Nobel Prize committee officially submitting you for consideration. I only ask that when you receive the seven figure sum of gold that you remember your poor poet friend, Gabriele.

I should also relay to you that Alessandra has transitioned from ardent letters drunk with passion to philippics rich in venom. As the cliché goes... Hell hath no fury... here is just one to give you a sense of her ravening madness.

Gabriele,

> *You are nothing but a womanizing fraud, an insincere charlatan! You write these beautiful poems about Love, but when Love is presented to you on a silver platter, you spit upon it. I have given myself to you completely, and yet you are as cold as an Englishman, a race that you claim to despise, yet whose sensibility you have adopted. You are not even worthy to possess a name like Gabriele Paterkallos, you should change it to J. Alfred Prufrock! This would be much more apropos for your frigid, cowardly, soulless self!! You selfish pig! I hate you!*

> *You have destroyed my life, my marriage, my reputation, and for what? Just for a brief interlude of pleasure to amuse yourself? May the Gods curse you for your demonic behavior! You are a devil with no hope for redemption, and may you burn in Hades for eternity! You claim to have a beautiful soul, but I have never yet met anyone in my life with an uglier soul!*

Your name now rips a fissure through my very heart.
Curses upon you! Curses!

Despisingly,

Alessandra

What does one do but ignore such puerile rantings? She knew full well that she was stepping into a hornet's nest the moment that our lips touched by the Colosseum; rather on second thought, the moment that she penned an effusive letter while married to another!

Need I remind her that it was *she* who pursued *me*, not the other way around, but alas, women are adroit masters of revisionist history, always ready to cast themselves as blameless victims in matters of love or lust. This woman need not seek a therapist, as I think a few novels from Danielle Bronze would assuage her furor. I've never read a popular novel, and I never intend to, but I do think that it would do this one some good, don't you agree?

-Gabriele, the pursuer of novel Sensations,

November 13th, 2001

Il Mio Caro Amico, Odysseus,

I just received a check for $500 from YouthMedicale for the referrals that I've sent them thus far. They are doing very well, grossing about $15,000 a day with hopes to build up to $70,000; they have advertised in many of the lifestyle and fitness magazines, so I think that in time they will attain such a princely sum. I will use the $500 to buy books, meat, and strumpets, though on further consideration, I will save my gold since I can procure any number of women freely.

I have seriously contemplated never returning to university, simply taking odd jobs here in Rome to support myself. Though I have been critical of the American Cultural Institute of Rome, perhaps I could apply for a position as a gardener on their grounds subsisting solely on tender kisses, dreamy rose-petals, and Homeric similes. I have too much pride to live in such poverty though, and am leaning towards returning to Florida – forcing myself to either be a proper bourgeois or to pursue this pharmaceutical opportunity.

You mentioned in your previous letter that you were dabbling in the sale of opium in Paris. Have you made much money from this? If you ever become imprisoned, I will have no way of knowing, so please advise your sister Stephanie to inform me, so that I can bring my army of heroic Greeks to Paris to free you, as a side excursion before we make our way to Nicosia!

Yesterday in the gymasia, one of the employees encouraged me to enter a bodybuilding show here in Rome. I demurred since I find the prospect of flexing in my underwear in some obscure high school gymnasia beneath me. I do enjoy being photographed for the fitness magazines, but posing for a motley set of applauding strangers, seems, well, strange.

It reminds me of an ancient male slave-sale set in the Roman world, where the men of a conquered nation were cleaned and oiled before being paraded about as pieces of meat, like well-muscled cattle, before the lusty eyes of aristocratic women, greedy lanistas, and land-owning patricians. Maybe I will reconsider my position however, as some friends are eagerly participating in this event. If you ever do come to Rome, we will train like Homeric Greeks whether I decide to compete or not. Your body, Odysseus, must remain as beautiful as your mind and soul.

-Gabriele, prophet of Kalon,

November 16th, 2001

Dear Odysseus, sailor on the wine-dark sea,

     I write to share some good news! I am going to Sicily tomorrow for a short odyssey. In my dithyrambic excitement, I have composed a poem.

Ode To Sicilia

I'm going to Magna Graecia!
Catania, Sicilia
To be precise.
'The Beautiful Land!'
So very far from Manhattan
and from London, England.

I'm going to Magna Graecia!
Ah, the isles of Sicily!
Favignana – Linosa and Lampedusa.
The very lifeblood of ancient Poetry!
Let me come
to be one
with your illustrious Beauty!

I'm going to Magna Graecia!
Oh, dark-skinned daughters of Sicilia:
Children of the once mighty Moors.
Whose glances are stolen from Tosca,

slayer of craven Scarpia.
And whose kisses are like winged daggers
dripping with the flowing blood of Aetna:
Savage and primal –
Full of scalding lava,
Yet somehow still irresistible!

Oh, my Sicily!
A tiny glimpse of timeless Graecian Glory!
A muted glimmer of fallen Roman Beauty!

-Gabriele Siculus

November 17th, 2001

Dear Odysseus, godlike man,

The trip to Sicily fell through at the last minute, and as you can imagine, I am crestfallen! I am drowning my sorrows in the flesh of a new lover, Adelina, hailing from Cordoba in the Andalusian region of Spain. I adore the darkened hue of her flesh, as if she has somehow managed to capture the potent power of the sun just beneath her skin! While we devour our bodies like famished cheetahs finally given sustenance, we listen to the savage 'cante jondo' (deep song) music sung in the caves of Andalusia by gypsies. You must not confuse it with its commercialized cousin, flamenco, as 'cante jondo' is so feral that it makes flamenco sound as tame as an emasculated Anglican choir. Adelina refuses to refer to me as Gabriele, addressing me only as 'poeta,' both when we are in 'the act,' and otherwise. How poetic it is Odysseus to hear *'Oh poeta! Oh poeta!'* bellowed throughout the apartment in wild paradisiacal singing.

Before this 'toreadora' arrives, I always scatter the crushed petals of a crimson primrose upon the satin sheets –

transforming the bed into a kind of profaned pagan altar devoted exclusively to the worship of sensual pleasure. Oh, the unbridled, unrestrained pleasure that life offers, if one only has the audacity to seize it! *Oh, the Pleasure! The Pleasure!*

Adelina is a true gypsy princess when she enters the room crowned in her voluptuous coronet – a coronet set with exotic coral, purple pearls, and colored flowerets. One does not know whether to worship her or ravage her. Adelina's full breasts are so well-wrought, like a perfectly halved parabola stitched with the riches of Persia, that it seems as if Praxiteles himself spent half a century devoted exclusively to their rendering. We plan to spend the entire afternoon drinking wine and worshipping our shapely bodies until we fade into a world of dreams and darkness. I have only these few minutes to write to you since she has returned to her flat to fetch her 'cante jondo' music.

Adelina is incredibly delicious, but she is just a transient plaything for me; just something to assuage my gnawing ennui. Our time together shall be as fleeting as a phosphorescent flare of cannon-fire in the evening air – as evanescent as a spiraling scent of Asian incense – yet as pleasant as a shudder of pleasure. And though our coupling will be very brief, it will seethe with such sensuous passion that the Olympians themselves will be offended! Sometimes I have the urge to mark Adelina with my fervent kisses, leaving a permanent bite-mark on her inner thigh or her lower back. Part of this is to claim my territory like a possessive lion, but I also dream of doing this so that she will never forget our furious liaison. When I return to America, it is unlikely that I will ever see her again, and in all likelihood, she will live a common life: marrying a successful bourgeois, having children, and such.

But I always want her to remember our Dionysian affair, to remember the immense amount of sensual pleasure that I gave her. I imagine Adelina 11 years from now stepping from the shower, seeing her love-wound reflected in the mirror, and softly running her fingers upon her scar, a scar the color of scarlet inset in violet. She will dream that her soft caresses are mine – given completely to nostalgia, to deep and profound emotion: closing her eyes to reminisce about our savage kisses, longing to once again be young, beautiful, and free – living solely for the pursuit of pleasure and passion. But just before she is totally consumed by her poetic fantasy, her young daughter will run into the room, jarring her back to reality. Adelina will undoubtedly smile, kiss her daughter gently on her forehead, and dutifully go about her day, enriched by both her impassioned memory, and the angelic smile of her innocent princess.

I hear a faint rattling at the door, so I must leave you now. I cannot wait to throw myself upon my Spanish plaything like a drunken comet fueled by sonatas of lightning – petunias colored in moonlight – and azaleas covered in sparkled sunlight. *Long live Odysseus Pane! Long live Gabriele Paterkallos! Viva Poesia! Viva To Kalon!*

-Gabriele, seducer of Spanish gypsies,

November 20th, 2001

Dear Odysseus, man of vast experience,

We must plan to travel to exotic places together, Odysseus: Morocco, Tunisia, Algeria, Malta, Andalusia, and other far-flung locales in the Mediterranean. I cannot add Turkey to this list, since I have taken an oath before Zeus himself that I will only step foot there in the pursuit of a beautiful death facing The Barbarians in hand to hand, chest to chest, eye to eye combat. But perhaps I should break this vow, cultivating a life of luxury, beauty, and 'idoni,' deep in the heart of Asia – spending my days in my seraglio, idling in an opium haze, stroking the soft cheeks of my soft-eyed sultanas, while gazing at the lovely Bosphorus. Why not, my friend? The modern Greeks are veritable cowards, intent on protesting against the influence of foreign bankers, having no real interest in becoming high-hearted heroes once again. So then, let us become debauched Ottomans until there is something heroic to pull us away from this dissipated lifestyle, a lifestyle rich in women, opium, and the drunken-songed Tulum. *Oh, the Pleasure! The Pleasure!*

But let us now leave Asia returning to immortal Hellas. Yesterday one of my Italian women mocked me for listening to Greek music, since I do not understand much Greek. She profoundly misunderstands my soul, for I do not listen to the music for the language, but for the limitless passion of the songs. She had wanted to play some popular music, and I told her that if she did such a barbarous thing that she could simply leave. I cannot allow the insipid songs listened to by the lifeless, passionless Anglo-Americans infect my herculean, Homeric soul.

My interest in all things Greek is not simply a strain of nativism, as my enemies will certainly claim, but rather, it springs from a devout devotion to The Beautiful. Just as the Englishman, John Keats, a man who spoke little to no Greek, either demotic or Attic, was so inspired by Grecian aestheticism that he composed *'Ode on a Grecian Urn'* and *'On first looking into Chapman's Homer.'* I personally find it impossible for a man to take a serious interest in beauty without also becoming immersed in the ideals of Hellenism, for no culture has adored The Beautiful more than the Greek. Do you not agree? Tell me, Odysseus, what other civilization would wage a ten year war, not for gold, glory or land, but for the ideal of beauty?

And to further illustrate my point, allow me to proffer the following example: were it to suddenly come to light that I had not a single drop of Grecian blood flowing through my veins, my passion for Hellenism would not wane in the least, for it is a conscious intellectual decision, not merely a happenstance of birth. It is not enough to simply be born a Hellene (Ελλην), one must *become* Hellenic (Ελληνικόζ). Now allow me to completely contradict my previous statement. The other evening while in rapt contemplation for a proper epitaph, I came to the conclusion that the only fitting choice for me would be the laconic *'Here lies a Greek,'* since no other English word fully encapsulates the description of poet, philosopher, scholar, warrior, adventurer, lover – and lover of beauty, truth, passion, and knowledge.

You had asked in your previous letter about my literary agenda after my poetry collection is published. I am always a moment away from renouncing literature entirely to become a full time gardener or a purveyor of narcotics, but if I do write again, I think that I will embark upon a series of dialogues in the Platonic manner (of, or relating to Plato, not an intellectualized love), or maybe a duo of tragedies – *'Oedipus Moira'* and *'Godot and Juliet'* – for the festival of Dionysus.

Allow me to now compliment you in the guise of unsolicited advice, or should it be, allow me to offer you unsolicited advice in the guise of a compliment? (As you can see I am very tired) Anyways, let me proceed with the thought: your prose is so very beautiful that I think you owe it to yourself and to the Pierian Muses to pen a collection of poesia. You will not derive much gold from this pursuit, but you will be garlanded in the rose-red roses of Arcady; also, I think that it would add a certain 'gravitas' to your name further improving your chances of winning the Nobel Prize.

Oh Odysseus, with every passing moment, I'm becoming more and more fatigued with the pursuit of sensual pleasure. None of my women understand my soul like the ancient poets. And besides, I've given all of my passion to poesy that I have little left for my own life.

-Gabriele, child of the Muses,

November 21st, 2001

Dear Odysseus, murderer of Democoon,

Nothing terrifies me more than prolonged silence. That is all. Now, go about your day.

-Gabriele, slave of the Lyra,

November 22nd, 2001

Dear Odysseus, sacker of citadels,

It is Thanksgiving back in the good ole U S of A – how I crave a heaping plate of Turkey and mashed potatoes washed down with a few sugary sodas. Yet, here I am, having just finished another feast of pasta and wine. I've told you before that I do miss the meat-centric diet of America, and I find myself drinking many more protein-shakes here so as to tend to the demands of my ever-growing physique.

I am just relaxing now – gazing at the street below, at the Italians as they take their customary passiegata, while I listen to the crystalline voice of Andreas Puccari before settling in to some reading for the evening. I was contemplating trekking into the *Campo dei Fiori* to pluck a pretty young flower from the flower-laden field, but I have decided to remain hunched over a book like a snarling old monk. I have not yet determined if it will be Vasari or Boccaccio, but either will suffice.

Though sometimes I hesitate to even open my books, for I feel that at the very moment I begin to read, I renounce life, ending any possibility for experience that day, escaping into the private realm of the mind. Yet, the incessant guilt works both ways, for when I am immersed in the pleasures of worldly sensations, be it in the carnal caress of a young nymph, the final flare of an occidental fire, or the sultry sight of a dew-imbued petal, I feel that I should be chained to my desk engaged in intellectual endeavors. I have lived far too passionately, Odysseus, to be as well-read as I should be. As you can see, I crave both sensation and knowledge equally, but cannot fully give myself to either. Do you also suffer from this torment, Odysseus?

This afternoon as I was dreaming of the future war in Cyprus, I found myself longing for a forgotten time. Though I understand the necessity for a government to develop innovative weapons, I lust for an era when a battle's outcome was decided by individual heroism, not by superior technology. Now, do not misconstrue my statement, labeling me a Luddite, for I realize the imperative of the US government to continue on the path of weapons development, for I do foresee a future conflict between the West led by the US and her allies against a Chinese-Arabian alliance, which will be decided mainly by technology – unseen men deep in the bowels of the earth on disparate hemispheres feverishly pressing buttons, and perhaps whomever pushes the buttons faster will be the victor.

How far that particular scenario is from Achilles glaring at Hector, breaker of men, across the sandy plains of Troy; and to be frank, Odysseus, the modern Achilles is not a hulking God, but a slim bespectacled mechanical engineer. But in my conflict against the Turks, I dream that it would be decided by courageous men, not soulless machines. I would sign a blood oath before Zeus himself with the barbarian commander abjuring modern weapons, allowing each army only the use of spears, swords and shields. Let his 30,000 assembled barbarians stand against my 300 Greeks and philhellenes, with the strongest tasting the sweet spoils of victory! *Oh Nike!*

If the Turks were wise they would simply send an assassin to Rome to murder me before I am able to raise my Grecian army. Were I in their position, I would pluck the most beautiful Circassian lass from some obscure village – let us name her Dünya Güzeli – sending her to Rome to properly seduce me before cutting my throat with a shard of sharpened glass. Mounting me like some untamed mare, hungry for mating, with her flowing hair flaring like the wings of singing angels – like a sheer curtain whipped by the western wind – like thin stalks of silken gold, we would jointly hunt for the elusive state of ecstatic bliss. And as we simultaneously climaxed, with me filling her womb with ambrosial ichor, she would savagely slit my throat – my blood coloring our entwined bodies like a gushing estuary flooding a hardened quarry.

Just before expiring I would hear her weeping, suddenly realizing that she has fallen in love with me. Overcome with passionate despair, she would then fatally pierce her breast, coming to softly rest upon my chest, with us suffering our death-throes simultaneously, before Charon ferried us to the dark depths of Hades where we would spend eternity partaking in the pleasure of our youthful bodies! Oh, what a poetic death that would be, Odysseus!

-Gabriele, vanquished by Dünya Güzeli,

November 25th, 2001

Dear Odysseus, avenger of Leucus,

 I am writing to you after a disappointing evening. Well, heroic for some, but disappointing for me, since I had thought that a beautiful death fast approached. I was idling for four hours in Piazza Santa Maria in Trastevere, sipping espresso, people-watching, reading here and there, when suddenly I glimpsed two dark-tressed goddesses entering the piazza, their ruby cheeks glimmering under the glinting moon. I assumed these oriental beauties to be either Egyptian, Persian, or something of the sort.

 I stared at them for some time, observing their movements, and their mannerisms, before I approached the fairer of the two, saying: 'Excuse me, can you please cease running your fingers through your hair in between sips of your wine?' She paused for a second, taken aback by my brazen 'attack.' 'How dare you! Why would you ask such a ridiculous thing of me? I can do as I please. I am a free woman.' I responded with a devilish grin, 'It was only a request, mi amor, not a demand, for every time that you run your delicate fingers through your rosy-fingered tresses, you inspire tremendous furies and sufferings within my soul. I only ask that you pity a man such as myself, a man with a heightened sensitivity to beauty, a man who suffers from the excesses of passion.'

 She smiled slightly – paused – looked at her companion – giggled a bit, answering, 'Well, I will only consent to such a rude request, if you have a glass or two of wine with us. My name is Dünya and this is my sister, Hatadje. We are from Istanbul and are here in Rome for two more days before returning to Turkey.' As soon as I heard the name Dünya, my eyes lit up like a flaming star flitting among moonlit pyres – like a seven-stringed lyre singing of Orpheus – like a running river of shimmering topaz. Finally, I thought to myself, the Turks had taken notice of me, so alarmed by the threat that I presented, that they had no choice but to send their famous female assassin, Dünya Güzeli, to murder me, granting me a glorious death! I smiled from ear to ear like a man who has just assumed his inheritance. We engaged in about twenty minutes of common banter, before Hatadje retired to their hotel room complaining that she was exceedingly tired from a long day of touring.

This left Dünya and I alone, which had to be part of their initial plan all along; they knew that I would be baited in by their Asiatic beauty, unable to resist them, hungering for their Turkish kisses. The moon shone resplendently above us – its splendid aureola seemed suffused with stolen aurorean light. After a few more glasses of vino, Dünya and I ambled about the streets of the Trastevere under the wondrous moonlight, entranced by its golden corona, before returning to my apartment.

How excited I was, Odysseus, not only for the prospect of devouring my new Turkish plaything, but for the Romantic death that was soon to be mine! So, as we dueled like a duo of sparring pugilists, fighting for dominance, with her finally conceding to the stronger force, I kept thinking about my approaching finality. As soon as I could feel myself nearing bliss, being steadily overcome by her depraved kisses, I placed her atop of my glistening body, a body agleam with sweat and oil, ceding control to her ungovernable hips for a few minutes before powerfully filling her womb with crystalline honey.

And just as I finished, I bared my neck, expecting a glassy dagger to end my existence, but instead she simply kissed me softly, saying, 'Wow, Gabriele, that was delicious, exactly what I needed this evening.' Can you imagine how depressed I suddenly became!?!? This was not *the* Dünya Güzeli, but just a random Turkish tourist here in Rome. Being riddled with aphasia, I could not get her out of my apartment fast enough. I now write to you deep into the Roman night as the lyre weeps its savage lament to the refulgent moonlight – reflecting my present sentiment.

-Gabriele, The Fool,

November 26th, 2001

Dear Odysseus,

I have received terrible, terrible news today. Alessandra was found dead. Her family's gardener found her unconscious in the rose-garden with sheaves of my poems lying about. It is presumed that she poisoned herself with lye in the manner of the poet, Vachel Lindsay, but this has not been fully confirmed yet. What have I done, Odysseus? The blood is on my hands, and my hands alone! If I had never responded to her initial letter, or if I had eloped with her to some Grecian isle, none of this would have happened. What a truly horrid monster I am!

Every time that I pass a mirror, I see her blood dripping from my face. The Gods have indeed punished me for my sins. To atone for my transgressions against this poor, innocent woman, I should swallow lye in front of her tombstone, descending into Hades to rescue her, trading my soul for hers.

-Gabriele

November 30th, 2001

Dear Odysseus,

I have been in a state of depression, locking myself in the athenaeum, forsaking all forms of pleasure – forlorn as a spring-flower shorn of its petals. Please come to Rome to lift my spirits.

-Gabriele

December 5th, 2001

Dear Odysseus, bane of Thersites,

I am sorry to hear that you cannot come to Rome, though I do understand, as I know that you have deadlines to meet with the forthcoming release of your magisterial novel. I've been trying to comfort myself in the excesses of the flesh spending the last few days curled up with different women. I can't even recall their names, to be honest. It has lifted my spirits somewhat, but I cannot help but to regard myself as something of a murderer. If I had acted differently, Alessandra would still be alive; this harsh reality will always torment me.

-Gabriele, of the wounded Soul,

December 18th, 2001

Dear Odysseus, of the great war-cry,

I have finally broken through the dreaded doldrums and am once again pounding upon the lion-skinned drums of Bacchus. Life is too precious to allow myself to wallow in misery like a miser who has been viciously robbed of his possessions. I must turn the page on my past, looking forward, with my eyes firmly fixed upon the celestial gardens of lovely Olympus. And as such, to celebrate my birthday, I escaped to Umbria, to the *'Kallistos Vineyard'* in Orvieto, just an hour's drive from Rome. Since the weather has turned frightfully chilly, we remained inside the winery all day listening to the owners speak about the history of the region and the winery itself in between drinking healthy drafts of delicious wine.

I consumed so much wine that when I finally ventured outside, I espied three moons! Can you imagine my initial excitement, thinking that the Gods had blessed us with the presence of two new moons? How glorious that would be! Yet, as I sobered up somewhat on the jaunt back to Rome, I realized the folly in my earlier vision: seeing only the singular moon, which hung like a lonely tusk lined with ivory linen. Thank you, by the way, for your birthday wishes; they are much appreciated. Hopefully, I will be able to visit Paris for your upcoming birthday. Anyways, I must go now – I finally feel alive again, and have the urge to take a new lover. Ciao! Ciao!

-Gabriele, the one who dreams of three moons,

December 22nd, 2001

Dear Odysseus, builder of baroque similes,

Christmas is a wonderful time to be in Rome with the entire city decorated famously. I am a pagan, and sometimes a strident one at that, but I do delight in the wreaths, the trees, and the general *joie de vivre* of the Romans. Every man, woman and child greets you with a smile, and sometimes even a kiss. The joyous nature of the

Romani is nearly enough to convert me to the cult of the Galilean. But since I am a man who says 'yes' to life, to the pitfalls of despair, to the excesses of ecstasy, and to everything found in between, I cannot bring myself to convert to the sect of denial and death.

I do love spending time in the churches of Rome, which are veritable art galleries, with timeless paintings adorning their walls. Besides viewing the paintings, I love the aroma of incense, the silken sound of hymned Latin, and the angelic warbling of the choirs. I submit to you that I've spent more time in the churches of Rome than many professed Galileans. My personal favorite is the Church of San Ignazio, a baroque gem, rendered by Father Andrea Pozzo with the tromp l'oeil ceiling being the ne plus ultra of his masterpiece. If you ever do come to Rome, you must see this church. Furthermore, I've decided that whenever a modern like Gerry Staltzer begins yammering about the importance of Warhol, De Kooning, or sundry other 'barbaroi,' I will repeatedly make the sign of the cross imploring Father Andrea Pozzo to whisk me away into ravishing realms of baroque beauty.

-Gabriele, The Aesthete,

December 25th, 2001

Dear Odysseus, jet-setter,

Christmas was rather uneventful with my publisher Gianluca having the Romanian servant-girls cook for a small group of his English friends. Being cornered into stilted group conversation with no escape is one of my personal *bêtes noires*. I do not do small talk. I've always believed that a conversation is a private matter between two people. I long to disappear under the table when it becomes something of a performance, a verbal game, riddled with fake laughter, with the participants straining to outdo each other in matters of wit. I am not witty, being too introverted and broody, for such a thing, but as you can imagine the English are masters of repartee, hurling witticism after witticism at each other. After thirty minutes of enduring their strained performance, I excused myself, complaining of an upset stomach. I locked myself in my room until all of the players left the stage.

I've decided to return to university when the new semester commences on January 12th. You are probably disappointed with this decision since you have forsaken all forms of formal education. I feel that since I have an academic scholarship, I should fully embrace the opportunity, finishing in three years or so. After that, I can return to Rome, or anywhere else in Europe for that matter. Also, besides fulfilling my obligation to complete university, I have been making a decent amount of money sending referrals to YouthMedicale; this opportunity could be very lucrative dragging me by my bootstraps out of wretched poverty. If I remain in Roma, I will not be able to fully take advantage of the situation. I know that this news disheartens you, but hopefully you will respect my decision, a decision that I confess is more pragmatic than Romantic.

-Gabriele, the solipsistic brooder,

December 30th, 2001

Odysseus, skilled in talk and tactics,

I have been staying in Venice for the past few days with a lascivious German heiress, Karin Von Vauer, who is as dazzling as a garden laden with the gems of Helen – as spellbinding as the golden stems of astral cyclamen – and as mesmerizing as an oriental spell fallen from the eyes of the Cumaean Sibyl. She is a few years older than me and has spent the majority of her early twenties here in Italy studying Art History. Her family has a controlling interest in one of the premiere hotels in Venice, so we live for free and are treated as visiting royalty by the help. One negative word from Karin would result in their immediate dismissal, so they fawn and dote on us like a train of bowing sycophants in an oriental court.

Karin is a delicious little morsel, so petite and tight, with one of my hands nearly able to encircle her waist. She loves the contrast of my hulking body with her tiny frame, and I must confess that I do as well. I am 6'2" 220 lbs, while she is 5'1" 100 lbs, so I am a full foot taller, and good 120 lbs heavier: A lion mating with a pussycat, no? Before we met she was somewhat reserved in matters of the flesh, but I have awakened her darker inner desires – feeding her a few bites from Eden's forbidden apple, an apple that flowers every spring on the tip of my devilish lips. One could say that I have thoroughly corrupted and tainted this poor woman, but alas, it gives me such inordinate pleasure to introduce a young girl to novel pleasures. We have been shuttling countless Venetian courtesans into our imperial suite to sate our insatiable erotic tastes.

Role-playing as Antony and Cleopatra is her favorite game with the courtesans cast as the concubine girls. Karin wears a perfumed, feathered headdress, with her eyeliner extending outward towards her temples in the Egyptian manner. She stands naked save for a long-flowing, lustrous robe, a robe made from the finest finely-spun Venetian linen. The robe becomes slightly diaphanous when struck by the strong light of Helios. All of the garish color and Asiatic pageantry contrasts splendidly with the pale hue of her germanic skin, skin as soft and supple as Yemeni honey. When her body is fully prepared for pleasure, she is as lithe and lovely as white-armed Aphrodite, of the immortal charms.

I am, of course, always 'gymnos' with a thin sheen of shimmering olive oil anointed upon my skin; honeyed rose-petals are carefully placed upon my hardened flesh by the full-flushed handmaidens. I kiss them softly as they perform their carnal duty. And after we have satisfied our lusts, we have the assembled courtesans hand-bathe us in a handcrafted marble tub, a tub teeming with fresh milk, before sending them on their way, a few ducats the richer for their services.

When I am not in the arms of my white-armed goddess, Karin, I am generally to be found in the Accademia, surrounded by supreme beauty. Bellini stands out, specifically for his blues, deep and rich, suffused with the holy hue of the Tuscan sky, in its fleeting crepuscular flare. Veronese' *'The Feast in the House of Levi'* also resonates strongly with me, especially for Veronese' compositional mastery – his ability to fill his canvas with numerous figures, yet not have the work appear too busy. Titian's love of ancient mythology is endearing, especially to the pagan within me; he also deftly employs Bellini's brilliant blues, or one could say the 'Venetian blue,' since it seems that the entire Venetian school was enamored with this dreamy, celestial color.

Besides idling in the Accademia and discussing metaphysics with the Italian pigeons in Piazza San Marco, I also thoroughly enjoy my solitary walks through the city in the late evenings. Last night, I stood for a long while on the Bridge of Sighs, staring through the stone bars at the falling starlight, which fell upon my eyes like a starry simile streaked with divinity. The stars flashed and flickered like droplets of honey fallen from the wings of Eros, as he aimlessly glided through the gilded cosmos.

I could only sigh for the beauty presently before me and for the ruinous state of my soul. Is there any hope for me, Odysseus? Will I always remain this accursed demonic libertine, despised by society and the Gods alike? Am I beyond redemption?

-Gabriele, Caesar of Sea-Sodom,

January 3rd, 2002

Odysseus, wily Ithakan,

I have been sleeping for the past few days recovering from my excesses in Venice, of the renowned courtesans. I promise to write more very soon.

-Gabriele, of the tired limbs,

January 4th, 2002

Odysseus,

There is nothing left for me in this life, Odysseus. Yesterday, there was a peace deal brokered in Cyprus between the Greeks and the Turks! Can you imagine this madness? *Peace? Peace?* What am I supposed to do with peace? How was I not consulted in the matter? Were they not aware of my maps, my battle-plans, my wooden horse? How could they do this to me?

What am I to do now, Odysseus? I have spent so many of my days and nights lost in dreams of Cypriot glory! Now there is nothing great for me to accomplish. My life will become utterly common without some grand action to catapult me into the pantheon of Grecian heroes. Literature is not enough for me.

I am sitting here with a vial of lye, listening to the lyre, contemplating ending everything. With the death Alessandra coupled with this bit of news, I am inconsolable. All of my dreams have been dashed by strangers. Suicide can be a noble alternative to a compromised life, Odysseus: the Souliote women at Zalongo, the Jews at Masada, Cato the Younger, the disabused poet, Chatterton, all illustrate this.

There is something wonderfully poetic about opening one's veins – the ultimate act of defiance against other men, and even the Gods. One does not simply expire arbitrarily, allowing the whimsy of the Olympians to choose the time, the location, and the manner, but rather, one asserts control upon every aspect of one's death. I think that this is the only option for me. I will surround myself with my literary masterpieces, read a bit of Homer and Sappho aloud, before consuming the lye, awaiting the specter of death to cloak my eyes in her vicious veil of eternal darkness.

Though I would like to believe in the immortality of the soul, I remain unconvinced of an afterlife, and think that our earthly lives may be the totality of our existence. Were I to be assured of an afterlife, it would be much easier for me to imbibe this lye, but I worry that at the very moment that I drink this poison, a haunting, permanent finality approaches. Oh, convince me otherwise, Odysseus! Convince me of the immortality of the soul – how I long to believe – how I long to be Paul, instead of Saul! Oh wretched Gods, blind me in your holy light!

As I've been writing this letter to you there has been a persistent rapping at the door. Should I answer it, or just continue on with my planned suicide? I will flip a coin to determine my choice: heads for an immediate death, and tails to unlock the door. And here we go. . . . with tails being the result. So, one second, while I go to see who troubles me with their unwanted presence.

Oh my, Odysseus! Standing in the doorway was the most exquisite sight: a beautiful Venetian woman – intoxicating as wine and lovely as dawn – her scintillating skin shimmered like a thousand diamonds splayed upon a pond of ice – she was clutching a few sheaves of my poesia trembling with anticipation like a wounded fawn before a roaring lion. She presently awaits my appearance in the foyer. I cannot bring myself to swallow this lye, for there is far too much beauty in the world, too many moments of pleasure to devour. *Oh, the Beauty! The Beauty! The Pleasure! The Pleasure!*

-Gabriele, just Gabriele,